MELISSA

Francis Durbridge

WILLIAMS & WHITING

Cover design by Timo Schroeder

9781912582785

Williams & Whiting (Publishers)
15 Chestnut Grove, Hurstpierpoint,
West Sussex, BN6 9SS

Titles by Francis Durbridge published by Williams & Whiting

1   The Scarf – tv serial
2   Paul Temple and the Curzon Case – radio serial
3   La Boutique – radio serial
4   The Broken Horseshoe – tv serial
5   Three Plays for Radio Volume 1
6   Send for Paul Temple – radio serial
7   A Time of Day – tv serial
8   Death Comes to The Hibiscus – stage play
    The Essential Heart – radio play
    (writing as Nicholas Vane)
9   Send for Paul Temple – stage play
10 The Teckman Biography – tv serial
11 Paul Temple and Steve – radio serial
12 Twenty Minutes From Rome – a teleplay
13 Portrait of Alison – tv serial
14 Paul Temple: Two Plays for Radio Volume 1
15 Three Plays for Radio Volume 2
16 The Other Man – tv serial
17 Paul Temple and the Spencer Affair – radio serial
18 Step In The Dark – film script
19 My Friend Charles – tv serial
20 A Case For Paul Temple – radio serial
21 Murder In The Media – more rediscovered serials and stories
22 The Desperate People – tv serial
23 Paul Temple: Two Plays for Television
24 And Anthony Sherwood Laughed – radio series
25 The World of Tim Frazer – tv serial
26 Paul Temple Intervenes – radio serial
27 Passport To Danger! – radio serial
28 Bat Out of Hell – tv serial
29 Send For Paul Temple Again – radio serial

Also published by Williams & Whiting:
Francis Durbridge : The Complete Guide
By Melvyn Barnes

Titles by Francis Durbridge to be published by Williams & Whiting

A Game of Murder
Breakaway – The Family Affair
Breakaway – The Local Affair
Farewell Leicester Square
Johnny Washington Esquire
Murder On The Continent (Further re-discovered serials and stories)
One Man To Another – a novel
Operation Diplomat
Paul Temple and the Alex Affair
Paul Temple and the Canterbury Case (film script)
Paul Temple and the Conrad Case
Paul Temple and the Geneva Mystery
Paul Temple and the Gilbert Case
Paul Temple and the Jonathan Mystery
Paul Temple and the Lawrence Affair
Paul Temple and the Madison Mystery
Paul Temple and the Margo Mystery
Paul Temple and the Vandyke Affair
Paul Temple: Two Plays For Radio Vol 2 (Send For Paul Temple and News of Paul Temple)
The Man From Washington
The Passenger
Tim Frazer and the Salinger Affair
Tim Frazer and the Mellin Forrest Mystery

INTRODUCTION

Francis Durbridge (1912-98) was prominent among writers of mystery thrillers for BBC radio from the 1930s to the 1960s. As early as 1938 he found the niche in which he was to establish his name, when his radio serial *Send for Paul Temple* proved so successful that further Temple serials over several decades resulted in an enormous UK and European fanbase.

It was therefore natural, while continuing to write for radio, that Durbridge should join the rush of writers into the newer medium of television. The result was that in March 1952 *The Broken Horseshoe* became the first thriller serial on British television. Much later, in a published interview (*Radio Times*, 21 October 1971) Durbridge said: "Twenty years ago in the United States, a producer told me that I was wasting my time by not going into television. So that's what I did – I tried to build up a reputation with serials, since I'd vowed never to write a Paul Temple episode for television."

Melissa was Francis Durbridge's eleventh BBC television serial, transmitted in six thirty-minute episodes from 26 April to 31 May 1964, although it could legitimately be defined as his thirteenth because *The World of Tim Frazer* (1960/61) had consisted of three interlinked serials of six episodes each. The casting was superb, with Tony Britton (1924-2019) as leading man for the second time (his first being *The Other Man* in 1956); but it's impossible to resist mentioning the charismatic Brian Wilde (1927-2008), who before his long comedy runs as Prison Officer Barrowclough in *Porridge* and Foggy Dewhurst in *Last of the Summer Wine* played contrasting roles in Durbridge's *Portrait of Alison*, *The World of Tim Frazer*, *Melissa* and *A Man Called Harry Brent*.

The producer/director of *Melissa*, Alan Bromly, had since 1955 been the guru for most of the Durbridge television serials. Their television partnership began impressively with *Portrait of Alison*, and from then on they regularly confounded viewers with the many Durbridge characteristics that became so familiar – numerous red herrings, cliff-hanger endings to each episode, and the certainty that none of the characters should be believed whatever they might say.

Melissa was repeated on Mondays from 7 December 1964 to 11 January 1965, with each episode shown again on Fridays from 11 December 1964 to 15 January 1965; and it was screened again from 11 July to 15 August 1965. Not only did this make it the most repeated Durbridge television serial, but ten years later there was a new production - this time in colour, starring Peter Barkworth in three fifty-minute episodes from 4 to 18 December 1974, and it faithfully followed the original. But even this was not the end for *Melissa*, as much later in May 1997 there was an entirely new version televised on Channel Four written by Alan Bleasdale, consisting of five one-hour episodes with the story updated to the 1990s and its first half being a prequel to the original Durbridge plot. This was, incidentally, the only time that Francis Durbridge's name had strayed from the BBC.

In spite of the absence of Paul Temple, viewers were enthralled for nearly thirty years by the consistently gripping plots that made Durbridge the pre-eminent exponent of the thriller serial on UK television. There was no doubt that he was the master of the twist and turn, following the tortuous trail of a character caught in a web spun by a killer who remained concealed until the final episode. There was also a distinct element of "Britishness", which distinguished his thrillers from the numerous American television imports that relied upon "sock-in-the-jaw" action rather than sophistication.

Both of the BBC television productions of *Melissa* became available on DVDs. The original 1964 serial was eventually included in the box set marketed as *Francis Durbridge Presents Volume 1* (BBC/Madman, 2016), while the 1974 production had earlier been marketed by BBC/Acorn Media in 2007. The 1997 Alan Bleasdale version was released on DVDs in 2006 by Channel Four.

In spite of his Britishness, or perhaps because of it, Durbridge built an enviable reputation in Europe. His radio serials were broadcast in various countries from the late 1930s, in translation and using their own actors; and beginning with *The Other Man* (1959 in Germany as *Der Andere*) there was a swell of Continental television versions that attracted a huge body of viewers. So addictive was Francis Durbridge on both radio and television in Europe that German commentators defined his serials as *straßenfeger* (street sweepers) because so many people stayed at home to listen to them on the radio or watch them on television.

The German television serial *Melissa* (10 – 14 January 1966, three episodes) was a translation by Marianne de Barde, adapted and directed by Paul May; the Italian television version was *Melissa* (23 November – 28 December 1966, six episodes), translated by Franca Cancogni and directed by Daniele D'Anza; the French television version was *Mélissa* (29 June – 6 July 1968, two episodes), translated and directed by Abder Isker; and the Polish television version was *Melissa* (3 – 17 December 1970, two episodes), translated by Kazimierz Piotrowski and directed by Jan Bratkowski. Apparently there was also a Swedish television production of *Melissa* in 1966, and according to IMDb there was a Finnish version with the same title beginning on 13 June 1966 – but further details have proved impossible to verify.

As with many of Francis Durbridge's radio and television scripts, *Melissa* was novelised (Hodder & Stoughton, October

1967). The book was entitled *My Wife Melissa*, whereas it remained simply *Melissa* in Germany, France, Italy, the Netherlands, Norway and Slovenia. But in Sweden it was *Vem mördade Melissa?*, in Poland it was *Moja żona Melissa* and in Croatia it was *Moja žena Melissa*. And for British lovers of audiobooks, a set of four CDs of *My Wife Melissa* read by Greg Wise was marketed by AudioGO in 2013.

Melvyn Barnes
Author of *Francis Durbridge: The Complete Guide* (Williams & Whiting, 2018)

MELISSA

A serial in six episodes

By FRANCIS DURBRIDGE

Broadcast on BBC Television

26 April – 31 May 1964

CAST:

Melissa Foster	Petra Davies
Paula Hepburn	Helen Christie
Felix Hepburn	Kerry Jordan
Guy Foster	Tony Britton
Police Sergeant	John Bryans
Chief Insp. Carter	Brian Wilde
Don Page	Brian McDermott
Det.-Sgt. Gibbs	Richard Wilding
Dr. Swanley	Norman Scace
Joyce Dean	Elizabeth Weaver
Chauffeur	Sydney Dobson
Man in car park	Mark Powell
Duncan	Reg Pritchard
Jackson	Ian Norris
Tom Billings	Richard Aylen
Peter Antrobus	Martin Norton
Mary Antrobus	Carole Mowlam
Police Constable	Stanley Walsh
Manservant	Arthur R. Webb
Carol Stewart	Patricia Marmont
Harry Kirkland	Denis Cleary
Det.-Sgt. Heston	Lennard Pearce
Police Doctor	Clifford Parrish
George	Anthony Sagar
Man with dog	Edward Brooks
Mrs. Long	Elizabeth Craven

George Antrobus . . . . Michael Collins
Receptionist . . . . Ann Wrigg
Maid . . . . .Marjorie Somerville

A New Production
Broadcast on BBC Television
4 – 18 December 1974

CAST:

Melissa Foster	Moira Redmond
Paula Hepburn	Joan Benham
Felix Hepburn	Ronald Fraser
Guy Foster	Peter Barkworth
Det-Sgt Gibbs	Richard Borthwick
Det-Chief Insp Carter	Philip Voss
Don Page	Ray Lonnen
Dr Swanley	Lyndon Brook
Joyce Dean	Elizabeth Bell
Man	Pat Gorman
Duncan	Desmond Jordan
Jackson	Leonard Gregory
Tom Billings	Godfrey Jackman
Peter Antrobus	Robert King
Mary Antrobus	Zuleika Robson
Mrs Long	Ursula Hirst
Carol Stewart	Marcia Ashton
Truck driver	James Appleby
Det-Sgt Heston	Roy Spencer
Police Doctor	Alan Charles Thomas
George	Godfrey James
Man	Reg Cranfield
Mr Antrobus	John Horsley
Receptionist	Sheelah Wilcocks

EPISODE ONE

OPEN TO: The Living Room of a flat off the Bayswater Road, London. Night.

The Foster's flat consists of a living room, double bedroom, kitchen, and a large hall. The flat is well-furnished and there are several good pictures on the walls and an abundance of books. The pictures have been chosen by MELISSA FOSTER, but most of the books (and the untidy desk complete with typewriter, phone, manuscripts, etc) belong to her husband. Music from a record player is almost drowning the persistent ringing of the front door bell.

MELISSA, a striking woman in her early thirties, suddenly emerges from the bedroom and she goes out into the hall. She is preparing for a party. Lipstick in hand, cocktail dress unzipped, she looks annoyed and exasperated by the ringing of the front door bell.

As the camera pans across the hall we notice a mirror and a table with a brand new hat-box on it. MELISSA opens the front door.

PAULA and FELIX HEPBURN are framed in the doorway. PAULA is in her early fifties; wealthy, a shade common, and a little overbearing. FELIX is ten years younger than his wife and better mannered – a portly, faintly "chuckled-headed" man, who tries to disguise the fact that he lives on his wife's income. He wears a dinner jacket and is having trouble with his bow-tie.

PAULA: Melissa! Aren't you ready yet?

MELISSA: Darling, I've had a hectic afternoon. I had a
             fitting at six o'clock and the wretched little
             man wasn't ready for me … Come in, Felix!
             Come in! …

PAULA and FELIX enter the hall.

FELIX: (*Feeling his bow*) Melissa, my old darling,
             you look – wonderful. (*Felix hasn't a definite*

3

stammer, but there is, occasionally, a noticeable hesitancy in his speech)

MELISSA: I feel like hell.

AS MELISSA closes the front door she notices the new coat PAULA is wearing.

MELISSA: That's new ...

PAULA: Yes. (*Pleased; stroking the mink collar*) Do you like it?

MELISSA: Yes, I do, rather. But I'm not sure about the collar, Paula ... I'm not wearing a coat tonight.

PAULA isn't offended; MELISSA can do no wrong in PAULA's eyes.

PAULA: I didn't know whether to wear it or not, but it's such lousy weather. (*She suddenly notices the hat-box*) Not another hat!

MELISSA: Oh, it's nothing, darling ...

PAULA: (*Laughing*) Melissa, you buy more hats than any other woman I know – and you never seem to wear one.

They move into the living room.

PAULA: My God, the same old tune! Don't you ever get tired of it? ...

PAULA moves towards the bedroom.

PAULA: (*Calling*) Guy, we're here! Put a move on.

MELISSA: Guy isn't here, he hasn't come in yet.

PAULA: (*Surprised*) But we're supposed to be at Don's at eight o'clock.

MELISSA: (*Irritated*) Yes, I know. I know, Paula, but there's nothing I can do about it.

MELISSA crosses to the record player and switches off the music.

FELIX: Where is the old darling?

4

MELISSA: You tell me, Felix! (*A shrug*) He had an appointment in Fleet Street, that's all I know. (*Turning her back on them*) Zip me up, Paula.

FELIX steps forward and fastens MELISSA's dress.

PAULA: What's going to happen to Guy, Melissa?

MELISSA: What do you mean – what's going to happen to him?

PAULA: Is he going to get another job?

MELISSA: (*Trying to control her annoyance*) Of course he's going to get another job! Don't ask such stupid questions, Paula …

PAULA: Well, it's nearly a year since that "rag" of his folded …

FELIX: (*Trying to straighten his bow*) It wasn't a "rag", that was the whole trouble. If it had been a "rag" it would never have gone out of business. (*Pompously*) I said to Lord …

MELISSA: Felix, don't let's go through all that again, please! I couldn't bear it. (*Crossing to the bedroom*) We'll just have to go without Guy. He can join us later.

MELISSA goes into the bedroom.

PAULA looks towards the bedroom, then turns towards FELIX.

PAULA: You know what's eating her, don't you?

FELIX: No?

PAULA: Guy doesn't want another newspaper job. (*Nodding towards the desk*) He just wants to go on writing those books of his. The trouble is he doesn't make any money out of them, not worth talking about anyway.

FELIX: I'm not surprised. Have you ever read one?

PAULA shakes her head and FELIX pulls a wry face.

FELIX: You'd think the poor old darling was going round the bend.

There is the sound of the front door opening and closing. FELIX looks at PAULA.

After a moment we hear GUY's voice calling from the hall.

GUY: (*Off*) Melissa!

GUY FOSTER enters. He is a serious looking, introspective man, who is trying very hard at the moment to conceal the fact that he is in a bad temper.

PAULA: Hello, Guy …

GUY: Why, hello, Paula! Felix …

FELIX: Where on earth have you been, Guy? We'd thought you'd got lost.

GUY: Where's Melissa?

PAULA: She's in the bedroom – she's nearly ready …

FELIX: Put a move on, old Scout. This thing of Don's starts at eight o'clock.

MELISSA comes out of the bedroom; she carries her handbag and is ready for the party.

GUY: I'm sorry, Felix – I'm not going. I've been out all afternoon and I've got an awful lot of work to do.

MELISSA: (*Annoyed*) What do you mean – you're not going?

GUY: (*Turning; irritated*) It's a perfectly simple statement – I'm not going.

MELISSA: But it's Don's birthday; you accepted the invitation weeks ago.

GUY: Yes, I know I did, but –

FELIX glances nervously across at PAULA.

MELISSA: (*Angrily*) You shouldn't have accepted the invitation if you'd no intention of going.

GUY: But I did intend to go when I …

MELISSA:	This is the second party of Don's you've cried off!
GUY:	Nothing of the sort!
MELISSA:	Yes, it is. He threw a party last year when he won the Stirling Moss trophy and you …
GUY:	Oh, for God's sake – last year!

GUY crosses to the desk and irritatedly snatches the cover off his typewriter.

| FELIX: | (*To MELISSA*) Look – Look, old girl, I really think we ought to be making a move. |

MELISSA stares at GUY, ignoring FELIX's remark.

PAULA:	Now come on, you two! Stop this belly-aching!
GUY:	(*After a moment; turning*) I'm sorry, Melissa. I've had a perfectly rotten day, I just couldn't face up to a party tonight.
MELISSA:	(*Quietly*) What happened this afternoon?
GUY:	(*Evasively*) Oh – the usual nonsense.
MELISSA:	(*Irritated*) Well, what happened – did they offer you a job?
GUY:	(*Reluctantly*) Yes … (*Shaking his head*) It was no bloody good, not for me at any rate.
MELISSA:	(*Angrily*) No – it never is, is it, Guy?

MELISSA turns and goes out into the hall followed by an embarrassed FELIX and PAULA.

GUY hesitates, angry – undecided whether to follow them or not.

In the hall, Melissa crosses to the table, puts her handbag down on the hat-box, and opening the drawer in the table takes out a pair of men's gloves. The gloves are wrapped in tissue paper.

| MELISSA: | (*To PAULA*) I bought Don a pair of gloves. I hope they fit … I didn't know what on earth to buy him. |

7

FELIX is looking at himself in the mirror, trying to straighten his bow again.

PAULA: We had a brainwave, you'll never guess what we sent ... (*She notices FELIX*) Felix, for Heaven's sake, leave that bow alone, it looks awful!

FELIX: The blasted thing's always skew-whiff ...

MELISSA: Here, Felix ... Let me fix it for you.

MELISSA hands PAULA the gloves, and moving in front of FELIX starts to straighten his bow-tie for him.

GUY appears.

FELIX: (*Pleased*) That's better ...

MELISSA: There you are, Felix ...

FELIX: Thank you, my old darling ... (*Feeling the bow*) Bang on ...

MELISSA takes the gloves from PAULA, ignoring GUY.

FELIX: Well – are we ready, everybody?

MELISSA opens the front door.

PAULA: (*To GUY*) My God, my husband's bright, isn't he? We've been ready since seven o'clock.

GUY: (*To MELISSA; quietly*) I'm sorry, Melissa.

MELISSA turns and looks at GUY; she hesitates.

MELISSA: Have you had anything to eat?

GUY: Yes, I dropped into a pub and had some sandwiches.

MELISSA: There's some cold ham in the fridge.

GUY: Don't worry, I'll be all right.

MELISSA: I wasn't worried, I just wanted to make sure you wouldn't go hungry ... Come on, Paula ...

MELISSA goes out.

FELIX: Take – take care of yourself, old Scout.

PAULA: Bye-bye, duckie. Be good.

GUY: Good night, Felix ... Have a good time, Paula ...

8

WHEN FELIX and PAULA have gone, GUY closes the front door and stands for a while deep in thought. He takes a packet of cigarettes from his pocket and slowly lights one. He is putting his lighter away when he suddenly notices MELISSA's handbag on the hat box. He picks it up and looks towards the front door, realising, of course, that his wife has forgotten it – then with a shrug he replaces the bag on the hat box and goes back into the living room.

CUT TO: The Living Room of GUY FOSTER's Flat. Later the same night.
GUY is sitting at the desk working on his novel. His jacket is over the back of his chair and there is an ashtray full of cigarette ends near the typewriter. GUY picks up this ashtray and is about to empty the contents into the waste-paper basket when the phone rings. We hear MELISSA's voice immediately the receiver is lifted. It is obvious that her mood has changed; she sounds pleasant now, quite gay in fact. (We do not see her during this phone conversation.)

MELISSA: (*On the other end of the phone*) Is that you, Guy?

GUY: (*Surprised*) Oh, hello, Melissa!

MELISSA: How's it going, darling?

GUY: What?

MELISSA: (*Laughing*) The book!

GUY: Oh – it's not.

MELISSA: Guy, I'm at Don's and I've met a frightfully interesting man called Walter Voss. You've probably heard of him, he's the man who owns …

GUY: (*Interrupting MELISSA*) Walter Voss! Of course I've heard of him, for God's sake! He owns half Piccadilly – the half he doesn't own he's pulling down.

9

MELISSA:	(*Amused*) Well, darling, listen – I've been talking to him about you, and he's terribly interested and wants to meet you …
GUY:	What – tonight?
MELISSA:	Yes; he's invited half a dozen of us back to his house. I said you'd join us there.
GUY:	But why on earth should a man like Voss want to meet me?
MELISSA:	He's talking about buying a magazine and he wants to find out what makes … (*Laughing*) Look, darling, don't argue, just take this address down …

GUY picks up a pencil and pad.

GUY:	Okay – go ahead …
MELISSA:	Roxford House, Clinton Mews, Regent's Park.
GUY:	Rox … R – O – X …?
MELISSA:	That's it. We'll be leaving here in about twenty minutes … see you later. (*Suddenly*) Oh, Guy, I almost forgot. I left my handbag behind …
GUY:	Yes, I know, it's on the hat box in the hall …
MELISSA:	Bring it with you, darling. Now don't forget …
GUY:	Yes, all right. Oh – how's Don?
MELISSA:	He's fine.
GUY:	Was he annoyed because I didn't show up?
MELISSA:	No, of course not. You'll see him later. Don't forget my handbag.

MELISSA rings off.

GUY replaces his receiver and looks at the address he has scribbled on the pad. He gives a little shrug, glances at his watch, picks up his jacket, slips the cover over the typewriter, and after tidying up the mass of papers on his desk goes out into the hall.

The camera pans GUY as he puts on his jacket and crosses the room.

In the hall, GUY stops dead, staring at the small table. The hat box and handbag have vanished. GUY moves slowly across to the table, puzzled.

CUT TO: Near Regent's Park. Night.
GUY is driving his car; searching for Roxford House. He is peering through the car window at the various street names, unable to locate Clinton Mews.
Finally, with an obvious gesture of annoyance, he swings his car to the right and drives through a side entrance into the park.

CUT TO: Inside Regent's Park. Night.
About a hundred yards from the entrance a police car and ambulance are parked at the foot of a grass bank. GUY's car appears and draws to a standstill about twenty yards or so behind the black Wolseley.
A UNIFORMED POLICE SERGEANT is leaning against the door of the Wolseley, casually watching a group of men – police and stretcher bearers. The men are standing near a clump of bushes at the top of the embankment.
A tall, burly looking man – who is somewhat unsteady on his feet – suddenly separates himself from this group and moves down the bank towards the road. This is DETECTIVE INSPECTOR RONALD CARTER.
The SERGEANT has heard the closing of a car door and turns as GUY approaches him.

GUY: Good evening. I wonder if you could help me? I'm looking for Clinton Mews.
SERGEANT: (*Puzzled*) Clinton Mews?
GUY: Yes – Roxford House, Clinton Mews …
The SERGEANT shakes his head.
SERGEANT: That's a new one on me.
GUY: It's Mr Voss's place – Walter Voss …

11

CARTER arrives and we see now that he is carrying PAULA HEPBURN's coat over his arm.

CARTER: What is it, Sergeant?

SERGEANT: This gentleman's inquiring for a place called Clinton Mews, sir. I've never heard of it.

CARTER: (*To GUY; eyeing him with interest*) Clinton Mews?

GUY: Yes. Roxford House, Clinton Mews. Mr Walter Voss lives ... there ... (*He has recognised the coat CARTER is carrying*)

The INSPECTOR looks at GUY, then at the coat over his arm.

CARTER: (*Quietly*) You've seen this coat before, sir?

GUY: Why – yes – I ... I think so.

CARTER: Where?

CARTER holds up the coat so that GUY can examine it.

GUY: It belongs to a friend of mine. Paula – Mrs Hepburn. (*Puzzled*) At least, I think it does ...

GUY suddenly looks up, staring at the stretcher-bearers who are now bringing the body of a dead woman down the embankment.

CARTER: When did you last see Mrs Hepburn, sir?

GUY: Earlier this evening, she and her husband ... (*Tensely*) What's happened?

CARTER: A woman's been murdered – strangled. We had the call about twenty minutes ago. (*He looks at GUY for a moment*) I'd like you to come along with me, sir.

DI CARTER and GUY walk over to the ambulance. The stretcher-bearers are about to place the dead woman in the ambulance. The INSPECTOR nods to one of the attendants, indicating that he wishes him to remove the sheet covering the body.

The camera cuts to GUY's face as the man follows the INSPECTOR's instructions.

12

GUY:	(*Softly*) Oh, my God …
CARTER:	Do you recognise this woman, sir?
GUY:	(*Stunned*) Yes … (*Suddenly, tensely, covering his face with his hands*) It's my wife …

CUT TO: The Hall of DON PAGE's Flat in St John's Wood. London. Later the same night.

DON's party is over; the front door is open, and the hall is crowded with people saying "Good Night" to their host.

DON, a rather handsome young man in his late twenties, is standing next to PAULA and FELIX, listening to a departing guest tell a "funny" story.

| MAN: | … So the publisher looks at the young man and says: "I think your book's very promising. You tell a good story – draw interesting characters – and you've got a very dirty mind." … |

They all laugh and as the laughter dies down CARTER and a plain-clothes man – DETECTIVE SERGEANT GIBBS – appear in the open doorway. The INSPECTOR recognises DON.

CARTER:	Mr Page?
DON:	Yes?
CARTER:	I'm Detective Inspector Carter, sir. I'm looking for a Mrs Hepburn.

Puzzled, PAULA and FELIX instinctively step forward.

PAULA:	I'm Mrs Hepburn.
CARTER:	I'd like to have a word with you, ma'am.
PAULA:	What – what about?

CARTER hesitates, looking at the other people in the hall.

| CARTER: | (*Quietly*) About your coat. |

FELIX suddenly transfers his gaze to the SERGEANT; he realises that the man is carrying PAULA's coat.

13

CUT TO: The Drawing Room of DON's Flat. Ten minutes later.

It is a large, elaborately over-furnished room, with a bay window overlooking a corner of the park. There are several photographs of DON taken at Le Mans, Monza, the Monaco Grand Prix, etc.

DON, PAULA, FELIX and the two Scotland Yard officials, are seated and are discussing the events of the evening. PAULA has obviously been crying and both DON and FELIX look worried and distressed. We realise now, for the first time, that CARTER has a slight Scots accent and is a man to be reckoned with.

CARTER: (*Consulting his notebook*) ... Now I want to make quite sure that I've got this right, Mr Hepburn. You say that you and Mrs Hepburn picked up Mrs Foster at about half past seven this evening. On the way here Mrs Foster complained of being cold and your wife very kindly lent her the coat she was wearing. This coat ... (*He indicates the coat on the settee*)

FELIX: That's – That's right.

CARTER: Later Mrs Foster discovered that she'd left her handbag behind, and she insisted on going back to her flat for it.

FELIX: Yes.

CARTER: That, I imagine, was at about a quarter past eight?

FELIX: Yes – yes, I imagine so.

CARTER: Didn't you offer to run Mrs Foster home, sir?

PAULA: Yes, of course we did, but she said she'd already made us terribly late for the party and she just wouldn't hear of it. We dropped her at a taxi rank near Baker Street.

14

GIBBS:	Did she take a taxi, sir?
FELIX:	Well – yes, I think so.
GIBBS:	You didn't actually see her get into one?
FELIX:	Er – (*He looks across at PAULA*) No, I don't think we did.

PAULA shakes her head.

CARTER:	But Mrs Hepburn, weren't you surprised when Mrs Foster didn't return – when she didn't show up at the party?
FELIX:	We were very surprised. I telephoned her flat to see what had happened but – there was no reply.
CARTER:	(*Interested*) There was no reply?
FELIX:	No.
CARTER:	What time would that be, sir?
FELIX:	Oh, it's very difficult to say. Some – some time during the evening.
DON:	I should say it was about half past nine, Inspector.
CARTER:	(*To PAULA*) What did you think had happened to Mrs Foster? Did you think there'd been an accident of some kind?
PAULA:	(*Hesitantly; with a nervous glance at FELIX*) No, we didn't think that.
CARTER:	Well, what did you think?
PAULA:	To be perfectly frank, Inspector, we thought Melissa had made it up with Guy – her husband – and they'd decided to spend the evening together somewhere.
CARTER:	Made it up? Had Mr and Mrs Foster had a quarrel then?
FELIX:	No, no, not exactly a quarrel, but …

PAULA:	They'd had a "tiff" – just a friendly "tiff", Inspector. You know the kind of thing. Nothing serious.
CARTER:	And what was this friendly "tiff" about, exactly?
FELIX:	Well, Melissa – Mrs Foster – wanted Guy to come to the party and he obviously didn't feel like it – he wanted to work.
PAULA:	It was nothing. Really, Inspector.

CARTER looks at PAULA for a moment and then consults his notebook again.

CARTER:	This list you've given me, Mr Page; the people who were at the party ... Haven't you forgotten someone?
DON:	I don't think so.
CARTER:	What about Mr Voss – Walter Voss? Wasn't he here this evening?
FELIX:	(*Surprised*) You mean the millionaire – the property chap?
CARTER:	Yes.
FELIX:	(*To DON*) He wasn't here, was he, Don?
DON:	No, of course not. (*To CARTER*) I've a fairly large circle of friends, Inspector – unfortunately it doesn't include Mr Voss.

CARTER looks at DON, hesitates, then gives a little nod and closes his notebook. The SERGEANT rises.

CUT TO: The Living Room of GUY FOSTER's Flat. Early next morning.

A tired, dishevelled, and desperately worried looking GUY FOSTER is sitting in an armchair facing the INSPECTOR who is standing near the settee. There is an attaché case on the floor near where CARTER is standing.

| CARTER: | ... You're quite sure about the time, sir? |

16

GUY: I'm quite sure. As soon as I put the phone down, I looked at my watch. It was a quarter to eleven.

CARTER: (*Nodding*) And Mrs Foster said …

GUY: Look, Inspector, I've already told you what my wife said. I've told you three or four times!

CARTER: (*Politely*) Tell me again, please, sir.

GUY looks at CARTER for a moment, hesitates, then:

GUY: She said she was at Don's – Mr Page's – and that she'd met a man called Walter Voss who wanted to have a chat with me. She said a party of them were going on to his place; and gave me his address and told me to meet her there.

CARTER: Go on, sir.

GUY: She also said she'd left her handbag behind – it was in the hall. She asked me to take it along with me.

CARTER: But when you went out into the hall you found the bag had disappeared?

GUY: Yes – and also a hat box. (*Nodding towards the hall*) They were both on the table. (*Shaking his head*) I just don't understand what could have happened to them.

CARTER: Well, surely there's only one explanation, sir.

GUY: (*Rising; angrily*) You mean – you don't believe me? You think when my wife left the Hepburns, she came back to the flat?

CARTER: (*Bluntly*) That's what she said she was going to do, sir.

GUY: Well, she didn't!

CARTER: Mr Foster, I realise this has been a terrible shock to you, but I'm afraid there are certain things which just don't add up. For instance, I've questioned Mr Page as well as Mr and Mrs Hepburn. He doesn't know Walter Voss.

GUY: (*Bewildered*) But Melissa told me that he was at
              the party, she said she'd been talking to him
              about me and he ...
CARTER: (*Shaking his head; a shade irritated*) Mr Voss is
              in Nassau, sir. He flew there on Tuesday. And
              just for the record, Mr Foster, he lives in
              Brighton – he hasn't got a house in Regent's
              Park.

*GUY stares at CARTER for a moment then slowly sinks down
in the chair again.*

GUY: But I don't understand this. I don't see why
              Melissa should have lied to me like that. And if
              she wasn't at the party when she telephoned,
              then where the hell was she?

*CARTER picks up the attaché case and moves down to the
desk.*

CARTER: Mr Foster, according to what you've told me you
              spent the entire evening here – working at this
              desk?
GUY: Yes ...
CARTER: You had no visitors and you never left the flat –
              at least not until you had the phone call from Mrs
              Foster.
GUY: That's true.
CARTER: Yet Mr Hepburn tried to get this number at about
              half past nine and there was no reply.
GUY: He must have dialled the wrong number. I was
              certainly here – and the phone was okay because
              Melissa got through.
CARTER: Yes ... (*He looks at GUY for a moment, then
              opens the attaché case*) You're quite sure you
              never left the flat, sir, and you're quite sure Mrs
              Foster didn't return for her handbag?

GUY: Good God, yes! I've told you that. I'm quite
                sure.

*CARTER gives a thoughtful nod and then slowly takes
MELISSA's handbag out of the case.*

*GUY rises and crosses down to the desk, staring at the
handbag. CARTER looks at him.*

CARTER: Is this your wife's handbag?

GUY: (*Stunned*) Why – yes.

CARTER: It was in a ditch, about ten yards from –
                where we found Mrs Foster.

*The INSPECTOR opens the handbag and empties the contents
onto the desk. We see a powder compact, lipstick holder, a
torn piece of notepaper, silver pencil, cigarette lighter, a
bunch of keys, and various odds and ends.*

CARTER: Do you recognise these things?

After a moment GUY manages a nod.

*The INSPECTOR picks up the torn piece of notepaper and
unfolds it.*

CARTER: (*Quietly*) Tell me about your wife, Mr Foster.

GUY is still staring at the handbag.

GUY: (*Suddenly realising the INSPECTOR has
                spoken to him*) What did you say?

CARTER: I said: tell me about your wife, sir.

GUY finally takes his eyes off the desk.

GUY: What is it you want to know?

CARTER: Was she in good health? Had she consulted a
                doctor fairly recently?

GUY: (*Puzzled by the question*) Melissa? Yes, I
                think she was quite well. She never
                complained of feeling ill. Not to me, at any
                rate …

CARTER: The reason I ask is because I found this in her
                handbag. (*He holds up the notepaper*) It's a
                prescription … (*He looks at the prescription*)

19

	It's torn; the doctor's address is missing I'm afraid ... but it looks as if it was made out on December 12th ...
GUY:	That's just over a week ago.
CARTER:	Yes, just over a week. (*Examining the notepaper*) It's signed by someone called Swanley ...
GUY:	Swanley?
CARTER:	Yes ... (*Studying the signature*) Norman Swanley, M.D. (*He looks up*) Did your wife ever consult a Dr Swanley, Mr Foster?
GUY:	(*Puzzled*) No – not that I'm aware of. (*Shaking his head*) I've never heard of him.

CARTER looks at the prescription again.

CUT TO: The Consulting Room of DR NORMAN SWANLEY, Wimpole Street, London. Later the same day.

The room is bright, airy, and clinically clean – it is obvious to even the most unobservant visitor, that DR SWANLEY has a flourishing practice and is devoted to modern art and Swedish furniture as well as his patients.

SWANLEY, who now holds the prescription in his hand, is sitting behind his desk facing INSPECTOR CARTER. The doctor is a pleasant, bespectacled, "boyish" looking man in his early forties.

SWANLEY:	... Yes, this is my signature ... (*He looks at the prescription*) But part of the prescription seems to be missing ...
CARTER:	Yes, sir. I got your address from the phone book.
SWANLEY:	(*Glancing at his watch*) Well – how can I help you, Inspector?
CARTER:	I found that prescription in a woman's handbag. The woman – Mrs Foster – was

	murdered last night and I'm investigating the case, sir.
SWANLEY:	(*Recognising the name*) Mrs Foster?
CARTER:	That's right, sir. A Mrs Guy Foster. A tall, dark, rather good-looking woman of about …
SWANLEY:	(*Rising*) I know Mrs Foster! She came to see me about a month ago. (*He moves round the desk*) You say she was murdered?
CARTER:	Yes, sir – last night, in Regent's Park. She was strangled.
SWANLEY:	(*Shocked*) Good God! Why, that's terrible. A delightful woman too, I remember her very well.
CARTER:	What was the matter with Mrs Foster, sir?
SWANLEY:	The matter? (*Puzzled*) Why, nothing, so far as I know.
CARTER:	But I thought you said she came to see you, Doctor?
SWANLEY:	Oh, I see what you mean! No, Mrs Foster wasn't a patient of mine. As a matter of fact, she came to see me about her husband. He was the patient – not Mrs Foster.
CARTER:	(*Slowly; astonished*) Mr Foster – Guy Foster – is a patient of yours?
SWANLEY:	Yes, certainly.
CARTER:	Would you mind telling me all you know about Mr and Mrs Foster, sir?

SWANLEY looks at the INSPECTOR, presses a button on his desk, then returns to his chair.

| SWANLEY: | Yes, of course. (*He sits down*) But I'm afraid I don't know a great deal about either of them, Inspector. Don Page, the racing driver, is a patient of mine and one day Mrs Foster – who was a friend of his – told him that she |

was very worried about her husband. He advised her to come and see me. Incidentally, Inspector, I'm a neurologist, specialising in …

CARTER: (*Interrupting SWANLEY*) Yes, I know, Doctor. (*Smiling*) I looked you up. Please go on, sir …

SWANLEY: Well, Mrs Foster made an appointment and came to see me. She told me that her husband has difficulty in sleeping, was of a very jealous disposition, and frequently quarrelled with her for no apparent reason. She also said that he resolutely refused to see a doctor. (*A shrug*) She was a charming woman and I felt sorry for her – very sorry – but obviously there was just nothing I could do. About ten days later, and rather to my surprise, her husband telephoned, and my secretary made an appointment to see me.

CARTER: Did you see him?

SWANLEY: Yes, of course. I examined him, gave him a prescription – this one, I rather imagine – and arranged to see him again in about a fortnight's time. I think, if I remember rightly, the appointment is for one day next week.

A pleasant looking girl in a nurse's uniform enters from the outer office. This is JOYCE DEAN, the doctor's secretary. She puts an engagement book down on the desk and goes out.

SWANLEY: Thank you, Joyce.

SWANLEY picks up the book and opens it; he finds the page he wants and then looks at the prescription.

SWANLEY: (*Nodding*) Yes, just as I thought. This is the prescription. (*Consulting the book*) I gave it to Mr Foster the day I examined him. Thursday, December 12th. His appointment was at

three-thirty. (*He consults his book again*) I'm
due to see him again next week, on the 23rd.

*A somewhat perplexed CARTER slowly rises, thoughtfully
scratches his forehead, then takes a photograph out of his
inside pocket.*

CARTER: Doctor, I'd like to make sure we're both
talking about the same man. (*He holds out the
photograph*) Is that your Mr Foster?

SWANLEY looks at the photograph.

SWANLEY: Yes, of course. That's Foster.

CUT TO: The Living Room of GUY FOSTER's Flat. Day.

*GUY is sitting at his desk typing; he looks drawn and tired,
and it is obviously an effort for him to concentrate. The door
bell rings and after a little while GUY rises, stubs out the
cigarette he is smoking, and goes out into the hall.*

*We hear the opening of the front door and the sound of
voices.*

CARTER's VOICE: Good afternoon, Mr Foster. May I
come in?

GUY's VOICE: Yes, of course.

GUY returns with the INSPECTOR.

GUY: I phoned you this morning, but you were out.

CARTER: Yes, so I understand. What is it you wanted,
sir?

GUY: (*A shrug; despair*) I just wanted to know if
there was any news – any development?

CARTER: (*Looking at GUY*) Yes, there's been quite an
interesting   development,   Mr   Foster.
(*Pleasantly*) May I sit down, sir?

GUY: (*Indicating the settee*) Yes, of course.

*CARTER sits on the settee; crosses his legs and eases one of
his shoes.*

CARTER: I've had another talk with Mr and Mrs Hepburn, sir. I understand your wife had a pair of gloves with her, when she left for the party?

GUY: Yes, that's right. They were a birthday present for Mr Page.

CARTER: (*Nodding*) Have you any idea what happened to them?

GUY: No, I'm afraid I haven't.

CARTER: We found your wife's handbag, and of course the coat she was wearing – Mrs Hepburn's coat – but we didn't find the pair of gloves. (*He looks at his shoe and eases it again*)

GUY: Why are you interested in the gloves?

CARTER: For two reasons, Mr Foster. One – because they're missing. Two – because I've got a theory about them. (*He looks at GUY*) I think the murderer was wearing them, when he strangled your wife. (*Quickly, deliberately changing the subject*) However, I didn't come here to talk to you about the gloves.

GUY: (*Faintly irritated by CARTER's manner*) No? Then what did you come to talk about?

CARTER: (*Examining his shoe again*) The prescription.

GUY: The prescription?

CARTER: Yes – the one I found in the handbag. The one that was given to you by Dr Swanley.

GUY: (*Surprised*) Given to me?

CARTER: Yes …

GUY: But I don't know Dr Swanley!

CARTER: Mr Foster, I don't quite see why you should lie about this. There's no reason why you shouldn't have consulted a doctor if you weren't feeling well.

GUY: (*Angrily*) But I'm not lying!

24

CARTER uncrosses his legs and rises from the settee.

CARTER: Wasn't your wife worried about you, sir? Didn't she talk to Mr Page about you, and as a result of that conversation go and see Dr Swanley?

GUY: (*Bewildered; he shakes his head*) Not to my knowledge.

CARTER: (*Faintly annoyed; he doesn't believe GUY*) Didn't you, personally, consult Dr Swanley on the afternoon of Thursday, December 12th?

GUY: No! No, of course I didn't. I've told you – I've never met the man!

There is a pause.

CARTER: (*With almost a sigh of exasperation*) Well – he's met you, Mr Foster.

GUY who is shocked stares at the INSPECTOR.

CUT TO: The Main Entrance to a block of flats in St John's Wood, London. Day.

A 3.8 Jaguar is parked near the kerb.

A taxi drives up. GUY gets out of the taxi and is paying the driver when DON PAGE emerges from the block of flats and crosses to the Jaguar. He is wearing a dinner jacket. GUY turns – notices DON – and rushes across to him.

GUY: Don!

DON: (*Surprised*) Why, hello, Guy! (*Not quite sure what to say*) Guy, I nearly called round to see you this morning, and then I thought … perhaps … (*Sympathetically touching GUY's arm*) How are you, old boy? Are you all right?

GUY: Yes, I'm all right, but – I want to have a talk to you, Don … I've got to talk to you … It's important.

DON glances at his watch.

DON: I'm frightfully late. I'm supposed to be in Coventry at seven o'clock. The Midland people are giving a dinner for ... (*He looks at GUY; hesitates, then suddenly opens the car door*) Okay – jump in.

GUY gets into the car.

CUT TO: Inside the stationary Jaguar.
GUY and DON are sitting side by side in the Jaguar.
DON: (*A shade embarrassed*) ... I don't quite see what you're getting at, Guy?
GUY: I'm asking you if Melissa ever talked to you – about me, I mean?
DON: Yes, of course she did. We frequently talked about you, old boy.
GUY: No, I don't mean that. I mean ...
DON: (*Pleasantly*) What do you mean?
GUY: Did she ever tell you that I was ... sick?

DON looks at GUY, is about to say something, then hesitates.

GUY: Well – did she?
DON: Yes.
GUY: When?
DON: About five weeks ago. She came to see me one afternoon. She said you ... (*Hesitating again*)
GUY: Go on, Don ...
DON: She said you couldn't sleep, were constantly bad tempered and – she was very worried about it. I told her you ought to see a man called Swanley. He's a nerve specialist in Wimpole Street and ... Incidentally, Guy, did you see him?
GUY: No, I didn't and that's the extraordinary thing, because ...
DON: (*Interrupting GUY*) You should have done, old boy. He's absolutely first rate. My own doctor sent

26

me to him about a year ago. You remember that crack-up I had at Silverstone? The one everyone joked about. The bonnet came off …

GUY: (*His thoughts elsewhere*) Yes, I remember …

DON: Well, it shook me, old man. It really did. My nerve damn nearly went. I didn't say anything about it at the time, of course. Played it up rather. Bit of a lark. You know the sort of thing people expect from "Dicey" Don. But by God I was groggy – really shaken. If it hadn't been for this Swanley character, I'd have had it – so far as the Grand Prix is concerned anyway. (*He looks at his watch again*) Look, Guy, I don't want to seem rude, but it's nearly five o'clock now and if I don't …

GUY: (*Quietly; looking at DON*) Don, what did Melissa really say about me?

DON: (*Embarrassed*) I've told you what she said. She said you were always "on edge", couldn't sleep, and she was …

GUY: She was what?

DON looks at GUY and hesitates.

GUY: Go on, Don …

DON: (*Still hesitating*) She said she was frightened of you.

GUY: (*Shocked*) Frightened of me? Melissa?

DON: (*With a little nod*) Yes.

GUY: But why on earth should … (*Tensely*) What else did she say?

DON: Nothing. I've told you. She just …

GUY: Don, please! I've got to know …

DON: She said you'd changed. She said at times you were almost like – a different person. (*Watching*

27

GUY) She said one night you deliberately started a row and then – threatened to kill her.

GUY: But that's not true! I swear to you that … Don, you haven't told anyone else about this? You haven't told the Inspector what Melissa ….?

DON: Good God, no, of course I haven't! What do you take me for? (*Agitated*) Look, Guy, please let's talk about this some other time. I'll be back later tonight. Ring me first thing tomorrow morning, there's a good chap.

GUY hesitates, then takes hold of the door handle.

GUY: (*Slowly*) Yes, all right. (*He turns*) This Dr Swanley – you say he's in Wimpole Street?

DON: (*About to switch on the car engine*) Yes, I think t's 87 – I'm not sure.

GUY gives a little nod and gets out of the car.

CUT TO: A Corridor in DR SWANLEY's house in Wimpole Street.

At one end of the corridor stands the front door of the house, at the other end the entrance to the consulting rooms.

The door bell is ringing and JOYCE DEAN comes out of a room on the left and passes down the corridor to the front door. She opens the front door and finds GUY standing in the doorway, his hand on the bell push.

GUY: (*Tensely*) I want to see Dr Swanley, please.

JOYCE: I'm sorry, but Dr Swanley … Oh, it's Mr Foster, isn't it?

GUY: (*Staring at JOYCE; astonished*) Yes – yes, that's right.

JOYCE: But surely your appointment is for one day next week, Mr Foster?

GUY: I – I haven't got an appointment.

JOYCE: But didn't we make one a fortnight ago when you
           last saw …
GUY: (*Interrupting JOYCE*) I want to see Dr Swanley
           now – it's urgent!
JOYCE: Well – I'm sorry, but the doctor isn't here at the
           moment, he's at the hospital. He won't be here
           until tomorrow afternoon.

*GUY hesitates and looks at JOYCE who stares back at him,
apparently bewildered by his attitude.*

GUY: Tell Dr Swanley I've got to see him. It's very
           important. I'll be here tomorrow afternoon at five
           o'clock.
JOYCE: (*Taken aback, but forcing herself to be pleasant*)
           Yes … Yes, very well, Mr Foster.

JOYCE closes the door.

CUT TO: The Front Door of GUY FOSTER's Flat.
Evening.
*GUY arrives; he carries a copy of an evening newspaper. He
searches for his key – eventually finds it – and lets himself
into the flat.*

CUT TO: The Hall of GUY FOSTER's Flat. Evening.
*GUY enters, turns and closes the front door behind him.
There are several letters on the floor, and he stoops and picks
them up. He is looking at one of the letters when he suddenly
realises that music is coming from the living room. GUY
recognises the music – it is MELISSA's favourite record. He
drops the letters and dashes into the living room.*

CUT TO: The Living Room of GUY FOSTER's Flat.
Evening.
*GUY rushes into the room and crosses to the record player.
He stands staring down at it. After a second or two he looks*

up, wondering who has played this trick on him – and whether this person is still in the flat.

He turns and goes quickly into the bedroom. After a moment he comes out of the bedroom and crosses towards the kitchen – he looks tense; very overwrought.

Suddenly he stops dead, his eyes on the desk near the window. The camera pans to show what GUY is staring at. The hat box is on the desk and on top of it, spreadeagled, are the missing gloves.

END OF EPISODE ONE

EPISODE TWO

OPEN TO: The Living Room of GUY FOSTER's Flat.
Night.

INSPECTOR CARTER is standing near the desk examining the pair of gloves. The hat box has been opened and a hat – a frail, flowery creation – rests against the typewriter.

GUY stands watching CARTER as he slowly turns the gloves over in his hands.

CARTER: You recognise them?

GUY: Yes – they certainly look like the same gloves.

CARTER: And you found them here – on top of the hat box?

GUY: Yes, I told you. After I left Dr Swanley's place, I went to have a bite to eat. I got back here about half past seven. When I entered the hall, I heard music. It was the tune Melissa always played and for a moment I thought … (*He hesitates*)

CARTER: (*Quietly*) Go on, sir …

GUY: The gramophone was playing – someone had obviously been in the flat. I dashed into the bedroom.

CARTER: Why, sir?

GUY: To see if the person was still here, of course. It was when I came out of the bedroom that I saw the hat box and the gloves.

CARTER: I see. (*He looks at the gloves*) You've no idea where your wife bought them from, sir?

GUY: No, I'm afraid I haven't. I don't know anything about them, except that they were intended as a present for Mr Page.

CARTER: (*Nodding*) So I can take it that you were surprised – very surprised – when you found that the gloves and the hat box were still in the flat?

33

GUY: But of course I … What do you mean – still in the flat? Someone obviously took them away and then brought them back again.

CARTER: But why should anyone do that?

GUY: (*Faintly irritated*) I don't know why.

CARTER: But that's what you think happened?

GUY: Why, yes, of course!

CARTER gives a noncommittal nod and moves down to his attaché case which is on the settee.

CARTER: I had a phone call from Dr Swanley about an hour ago. He sounded puzzled – which doesn't surprise me. He says you insist on seeing him tomorrow afternoon.

GUY: I do indeed.

CARTER: Would you object to my being present at the interview, sir?

GUY: Of course not. Since the man's an obvious liar I should prefer it, Inspector.

CARTER: You still maintain that you haven't met Dr Swanley, sir – that you haven't consulted him?

GUY: I most certainly do!

CARTER looks at GUY, then picking up the attaché case sits down on the settee.

CARTER: Mr Foster, do you mind if I ask you one or two rather personal questions?

GUY: I was under the impression you'd been doing that.

CARTER: When did you first meet your wife, sir?

GUY: About three years ago. Paula – Mrs Hepburn – introduced us. They met on the boat coming back from Capetown. My wife was a South African. Her parents died about five years ago; she had no relatives, no ties in South Africa, so she decided to come over here and try her luck.

34

CARTER: Try her luck at what, exactly?

GUY: She wanted to be an actress; she'd played with an amateur company in Capetown and she thought if she came over to England she might break into films.

CARTER: Instead of which she met you and you got married?

GUY: Yes.

CARTER: I understand you were on the London Dispatch for a time, Mr Foster?

GUY: For almost nine years.

CARTER: What happened when the paper folded?

GUY: I was offered a job with another outfit, but I turned it down. I – I wanted to freelance.

CARTER: Was your wife happy about that?

GUY: Since you ask, no, not very – she wanted me to get a job.

CARTER: Was that a bone of contention between you, sir?

GUY: What?

CARTER: The fact that you hadn't a regular job?

GUY: (*Bluntly; facing CARTER*) We had several quarrels about it, if that's what you mean. But then we quarrelled about quite a few things. My wife was extravagant, stupidly extravagant at times. She bought more hats than any other woman I know, and yet she never seemed to wear one. But then I expect our friends have told you about our quarrels, Inspector.

CARTER looks at GUY, then opens the attaché case.

CARTER: Had your wife any money of her own, Mr Foster?

GUY: No; when we married she had three hundred pounds but that vanished a long time ago, I'm afraid.

35

CARTER nods and takes a ring, a pearl necklace, a pair of earrings, and a brooch out of the case.

CARTER: Do you recognise these?

GUY: Yes.

CARTER: Your wife was wearing them?

GUY nods.

CARTER: Did you buy them for her, sir?

GUY: Yes, well – I gave her the money. She'd never let me pick things for her – especially jewellery, she said I knew nothing about it.

CARTER picks up the brooch.

CARTER: How much is it worth, sir?

GUY: She bought it last Christmas. I gave her thirty-five pounds.

CARTER: (*Smiling*) And you think that's what she paid for it?

GUY: Why, yes.

CARTER: Your wife was apparently right, Mr Foster. I'm afraid you don't know anything about jewellery.

GUY looks at CARTER; puzzled.

CARTER: The brooch is worth three hundred pounds, sir. The earrings and the ring about nine hundred. The pearls are genuine, too – they're probably worth about two-fifty.

GUY: (*Staggered*) But that's absolute nonsense!

CARTER: It isn't nonsense, sir – they've been examined by an expert. The whole lot's worth not far short of fifteen hundred pounds.

GUY: But – but I just can't believe that!

CARTER: It's true, Mr Foster.

GUY stares at CARTER for a moment, then slowly picks up the pearl necklace.

CUT TO: The Breakfast Room of PAULA HEPBURN's Flat in Eaton Square. Morning.

PAULA and FELIX are having breakfast surrounded by a selection of morning newspapers. FELIX is wearing pyjamas and a dressing gown; PAULA a somewhat flamboyant housecoat.

The door bell is ringing but they are oblivious to the fact, being immersed in their respective newspapers.

FELIX: (*Suddenly looking up*) I say, old girl, that's the front door.

PAULA: It's probably the post. Let Dora go ...

FELIX: Dora, my sweetheart, is in Leamington Spa – sampling the waters. (*He rises*) Or whatever it is you sample in Leamington.

PAULA: Knowing Dora, it won't be the water.

FELIX goes out into the hall, and after a moment we hear the opening of the front door.

FELIX's VOICE: (*Surprised*) Why, hello, Guy! Didn't expect to see you ...

GUY's VOICE: Is Paula in?

PAULA recognises GUY's voice and, putting down her newspaper, rises from the table.

FELIX's VOICE: Yes, of course. Come along in! We're just having breakfast.

FELIX re-enters with GUY.

PAULA: Hello, Guy! How nice to see you, duckie! Have you had breakfast? (*Before GUY replies*) I'll get you some coffee ...

PAULA's manner is just a shade too sympathetic.

GUY: No, thank you, Paula. Please – I don't want anything. I've had breakfast.

FELIX: (*Embarrassed*) We've just been reading the papers.

37

GUY: Paula, I saw the Inspector again last night. You
            know that jewellery of Melissa's, well apparently
            it's real – it's worth quite a lot of money.
FELIX: Real?
GUY: (*Turning towards FELIX*) Yes – the brooch alone
            is worth three hundred pounds – the rest of the
            jewellery well over a thousand.
FELIX: Well, I'll be damned, old boy! Did you know
            anything about this, Paula?
PAULA looks at GUY; she hesitates.
GUY: (*To PAULA*) Paula, you must have known she was
            wearing real jewellery. You can't tell me that you
            …
PAULA: (*Nodding*) Yes, I had my suspicions, but I wasn't
            sure. I actually spoke to her about it once.
FELIX: (*Surprised*) Did you, old girl? When was that?
PAULA: Oh, about eight or nine months ago. She just
            laughed at me – treated the whole thing as a
            joke. (*A shrug*) I'm afraid she convinced me I was
            talking nonsense. Let's face it, they make pretty
            good fakes these days – and besides, I kept asking
            myself how on earth could Melissa afford to buy
            the real McCoy anyway?
GUY: Yes, that's exactly what I keep asking myself.
            (*Moving towards PAULA*) Paula, you were
            Melissa's best friend, she must have talked to you
            – she must have confided in you more than anyone
            else.
PAULA: (*Shaking her head*) No, that's not strictly true. I
            was very fond of Melissa, of course, but we were
            never close to each other – not really close. I never
            really knew what went on in that pretty head of
            hers.
FELIX: I don't think anyone did – except perhaps Don.

GUY: (*Turning towards FELIX*) Don?

FELIX: (*Without thinking*) Yes, I always think old Don understood her better than anyone else. (*To GUY; suddenly realising what he has said*) Apart from you, of course, my old dear.

PAULA: Incidentally, Don phoned this morning. He said you went to see him yesterday afternoon?

GUY: Yes, I did.

PAULA: About – Melissa?

GUY: Yes. The police found a prescription in Melissa's handbag, signed by a Dr Swanley. The Inspector questioned me about it. I'd never heard of the man.

PAULA: Well?

GUY: Well – apparently, some little time ago, Melissa was worried about me, so she had a word with Don. He advised her to consult this Dr Swanley.

FELIX: And did she?

GUY: Yes – at least Swanley says she did. Unfortunately, you just can't believe a word the man says.

FELIX: (*Puzzled*) What makes you say that, old boy?

GUY: He told the Inspector that I was a patient of his and that he'd given me the prescription. (*Shaking his head*) I've never even seen the chap.

FELIX: But why on earth should he say a thing like that?

GUY: I don't know why, Felix.

PAULA: (*Curious*) Guy, why was Melissa worried about you?

GUY: She thought I was ill.

PAULA: Yes, but – was that the only reason she was worried?

FELIX looks across at PAULA; obviously puzzled by her question.

39

GUY: No. (*After a moment*) She told Don she was
            frightened of me.
FELIX: Frightened of you? (*Shocked; moving across to
            GUY*) And did Don tell you that?
GUY: Yes.
FELIX: God bless my soul, what's the matter with the
            fellow! What a tactless thing to say to a chap
            when his wife's just ... Frightened of you
            indeed! (*To PAULA; emphatically*) Melissa
            certainly never gave us that impression, did
            she, old girl?
PAULA looks at GUY for a split second, then turns away.
PAULA: No. No, of course not.
*GUY watches PAULA as she deliberately busies herself at the
table.*
PAULA: (*Not looking at GUY*) Are you sure you
            wouldn't like some coffee, Guy?
GUY: (*Still watching PAULA*) Yes, I'm quite sure,
            thank you, Paula.

CUT TO: DR SWANLEY's Consulting Room, Wimpole
Street, London. Afternoon.
*DR SWANLEY is sitting behind his desk facing GUY and
INSPECTOR CARTER. GUY is standing glaring down at the
DOCTOR. A frowning, slightly bewildered INSPECTOR sits
in an armchair, legs crossed, fidgeting with his right shoe.*
SWANLEY: ... Mr Foster, we've been talking now for
            nearly ten minutes, and we still haven't
            reached any conclusion.
GUY: (*Angrily*) I've reached a conclusion! You're
            lying! You must be because ...
CARTER: (*Rising*) Mr Foster, please!
GUY hesitates, looking first at CARTER, then at SWANLEY.

GUY: (*To SWANLEY*) I met you for the first time ten minutes ago, when I walked through that door. (*Shaking his head*) Before then, I'd never even set eyes on you!

CARTER: (*Embarrassed; to SWANLEY*) Doctor, surely there must be a perfectly simple explanation for all this?

SWANLEY: There is a simple explanation, Inspector. Either Mr Foster has forgotten that he came to see me on the afternoon of December the 12th, or, for some reason or other, he wishes to convince you that he didn't see me. (*Nodding towards the door*) You've spoken to Miss Dean – my secretary; you saw what happened. She recognised Mr Foster and confirmed what I'd already told you. (*A shrug*) I'm afraid there's really nothing else for me to say, Inspector.

CARTER looks at GUY.

GUY: (*To SWANLEY; trying to control himself*) Very well, I consulted you. What happened?

SWANLEY: (*Puzzled*) What happened?

GUY: Yes.

SWANLEY: But you know perfectly well what happened.

GUY: I'm asking you to tell the Inspector.

SWANLEY: (*Quietly*) I have your permission to do that, Mr Foster?

GUY: Yes – of course you have!

SWANLEY: (*Nodding*) Very well.

SWANLEY opens a drawer in his desk and takes out his casebook. He consults it for a moment, then looks across at CARTER who has dropped back into the armchair again.

SWANLEY: When I saw Mrs Foster, she told me that her husband couldn't sleep. She said that he was

41

constantly "on edge" – those are her exact words – and that he had a very jealous disposition. I asked her what, precisely, she meant by that, and she said … (*He looks at GUY*) … that her husband had actually accused her of having an affair with someone.

GUY: But that's nonsense, I never for one second thought …

CARTER: (*Stopping GUY*) Go on, Doctor …

SWANLEY: A little while later, when I examined Mr Foster, I questioned him about this, and he admitted quite frankly that he was worried about his wife. He said that he had no real proof that she was sleeping with someone, but always constantly at the back of his mind, there was this terrible suspicion. (*He looks at the casebook and reads from it*) Question: Have you spoken to your wife about this? Answer: Yes. Question: Did you tell her that you suspected her? That you thought that she was having an affair with another man? Answer: Yes, I did, and she denied it. Question: And you choose not to believe your wife, Mr Foster, is that it? Answer: I want to believe her … I've tried to believe her … God knows I've tried … but it's just no use, Doctor   …

GUY stares at SWANLEY, then deliberately turns towards the INSPECTOR.

GUY: (*Softly; tensely*) But this isn't true! I never – not for a minute – suspected that Melissa was having an affair with anyone! Good God, the thought never entered my head …

42

CARTER: (*To SWANLEY, ignoring GUY*) After you examined Mr Foster what conclusion did you come to?

SWANLEY: I'm afraid I came to no definite conclusion, but I thought he was possibly suffering from obsessional neurosis. I made arrangements to see him again and gave him a prescription – (*He indicates the paper on the desk*) the one you found in Mrs Foster's handbag. It was a sedative; sodium-amytol.

CARTER looks at GUY who stands staring at the DOCTOR – tense, angry, shaking his head.

JOYCE DEAN enters.

JOYCE: I'm sorry, Doctor, but you're due at the Middlesex at half-past five.

SWANLEY: Is the car here?

JOYCE: Yes.

After a brief glance at GUY, JOYCE goes out.

GUY: (*Unable to control himself any longer*) You're lying! Everything you've said is just lies – a pack of lies!

SWANLEY rises. So far as he is concerned the interview is at an end. GUY stares at the INSPECTOR, at SWANLEY, then without saying another word goes out. CARTER picks up his hat.

SWANLEY: (*Quietly; tidying the papers on his desk*) I'm afraid he's a sick man.

CARTER: How sick?

SWANLEY gives a non-committal shrug and goes on gathering his papers together. CARTER goes to the door, then turns.

CARTER: Doctor ...

SWANLEY: (*Looking up*) Yes?

43

CARTER: In your opinion, is it possible for a man – a
              sane man – to commit a murder and know
              nothing about it?
SWANLEY: (*Looking at CARTER*) If Mr Foster murdered
              his wife – he knows about it, Inspector.

CARTER nods and goes out.

CUT TO: Wimpole Street. Evening.

*A standard "S" Bentley is parked outside DR SWANLEY's
consulting room in Wimpole Street. A uniformed driver stands
by the car waiting for the doctor. GUY comes out of the house
and is about to cross the pavement when he notices the car
and the chauffeur. The man turns, realises that GUY is
interested in the car, and their eyes meet. As GUY moves
away, he notices the car's registration number: N.S.100.*

CUT TO: The Living Room of GUY's Flat. Evening.

*GUY enters from the hall, having taken off his hat and coat.
He closes the curtains and then crosses to the typewriter,
which is on the desk. He reads the partly completed page of
his novel which is in the typewriter and, obviously disliking it
intensely, rips the sheet of paper out of the machine and
tosses it into the waste-paper basket. He puts the loose cover
over the typewriter and stands deep in thought, staring down
at the photograph of MELISSA.*

The phone rings.

GUY: (*Lifting the receiver; on the phone*) Hello …
              Guy Fraser speaking …

CUT TO: A Telephone Box in Curzon Street. London.

*FELIX is on the telephone. He appears nervous, a shade
tense.*

FELIX: Hello, Guy – this is Felix. Are you alone?
GUY: Yes, I'm alone.

FELIX: Guy, I'd like to see you. Will you be at home for the next hour or so?

CUT TO:
GUY: I'll be here all evening, so far as I know. Is anything the matter?
FELIX: No. No, I just … want to have a chat, that's all.
The door bell is ringing.
GUY: Just a second, Felix – there's someone at the door.

CUT TO:
FELIX: (*Quickly*) Guy, wait a minute!
GUY: Yes?
FELIX: I – I think perhaps we'd better meet somewhere else. There's a pub not far from your place – The Golden something or other   …
GUY: The Golden Fox …
FELIX: That's it, my old dear! I'll see you there in about an hour.

CUT TO:
GUY: (*Puzzled*) Yes, all right, Felix.
FELIX: Oh, and Guy – don't mention this to anyone, there's a good chap. (*He replaces the receiver*)
The door bell is ringing again. GUY thoughtfully replaces his receiver and goes out into the hall.
DON PAGE is just about to ring the bell again when GUY opens the front door.
GUY: (*Surprised*) Hello, Don!
DON: I wasn't sure whether there was anyone in.
GUY: I was on the phone. Come in!
GUY looks at the small metal deedbox which DON is carrying. They enter the living room.
GUY: Can I get you a drink?

DON: No, I don't think I will, thanks, old boy.

GUY looks at the deedbox again.

GUY: What's that?

DON: It's a deedbox.

GUY: Yes, I can see that.

DON turns and takes the box across to the desk.

DON: It belonged to Melissa. She asked me to keep it for her.

GUY: Melissa did?

DON: Yes ...

GUY: When?

DON: Oh – oh, about six months ago. Look, Guy – I bumped into Paula this afternoon and she told me about the jewellery – Melissa's jewellery, I mean. I think I can set your mind at rest about that. I've got a pretty shrewd idea where it came from.

GUY: (*Quietly*) Did you give it to her, Don?

DON: Me? Why, good heavens no! (*Laughing*) Women give me things, old boy, I don't go spending my money on ... (*He stops; looks at GUY*) ... Now wait a minute, there's something we've got to get straight! Melissa and I were friends – very good friends – but we weren't in love with each other and there was never any nonsense between us, never – in spite of what certain people might think. (*Facing GUY*) I hope you believe that, Guy.

GUY: Yes, I believe it. But – tell me about the jewellery.

DON: I'd better tell you about Melissa first. There's something you don't know.

GUY: What do you mean?

DON: She was a gambler. My God, what a gambler! She'd gamble on anything, old boy – horses, dogs, baccarat, roulette, two ruddy bluebottles climbing up a wall if she felt like it.

GUY: But how could she gamble? She hadn't any money of her own and everything I gave her she spent on …

DON: (*Interrupting GUY*) My dear fellow, I don't think you've quite caught on! Unlike most gamblers, Melissa didn't lose – she won!

GUY looks at DON; there is a pause.

GUY: She won?

DON: Yes.

GUY: You mean – she always won?

DON: Nearly always, old chap – it was fantastic!

GUY: (*After a moment*) How much did she win?

DON: Oh … heaven only knows …

GUY: But – why didn't she tell me about this?

DON: Because she knew perfectly well that you'd try to stop her from gambling. And you would have done, wouldn't you, Guy?

GUY: I don't believe this, Don! If Melissa had won a great deal of money I'd have been the first to …

DON: Then tell me: where did her jewellery come from?

GUY: You mean – she bought the jewellery?

DON: Of course she bought it! She had to do something with the filthy lucre.

GUY hesitates. He isn't sure whether he believes DON or not; he looks at the deedbox.

GUY: What's in this, do you know?

DON: No, I don't. She brought it to me about six months ago and asked if she could leave it with me. I wasn't very keen on the idea, but I knew what was going on and … (*A shrug*) Well, Melissa and I always helped each other out if we could. Last summer there was a girlfriend I couldn't get rid of and Melissa … Yes, well that's another story.

GUY: Is there a key to this?

DON: Yes – but I haven't got it, old boy.

GUY crosses to the desk, opens a drawer, and takes out a bunch of keys. He examines the keys, then looks at the deedbox.

DON: (*Indicating the keys*) Were those Melissa's?

GUY: Yes. These two are for suitcases … I don't know about this one … (*Looking at the key*)

GUY tries the key, and it opens the deedbox. DON joins him at the desk, curious about the contents of the box.

GUY takes a letter, a jewellery case, a folded sheet of notepaper, and a Swiss savings bank book out of the deedbox. He opens the bank book and looks at it.

GUY: (*Softly*) Good God …

DON: What is it?

GUY: (*Looking at the book*) It's a bank book … Melissa Foster … Geneva National Bank … Four hundred and fifty-two thousand francs …

DON: I told you, didn't I!

GUY opens the jewellery case; it contains a diamond necklace.

DON: Boy!

GUY: I – I suppose it's genuine?

DON takes the necklace and examines it. As he does so GUY looks at the folded sheet of notepaper.

DON: Yes, it's genuine all right. This thing must have cost a packet … (*He looks at GUY who is thoughtfully staring at the sheet of notepaper*) What's that, Guy?

GUY: (*Quietly*) It's an I.O.U., Don.

GUY puts the sheet of notepaper in his wallet and then picks up the letter.

A close-up of the letter in GUY's hand. Two words – "For Guy" are written on the envelope. GUY slits open the envelope and takes out the letter.

GUY's face is first puzzled and then startled, as he reads the letter.

DON watches as GUY slowly sits down on the settee, still staring at the letter in his hand.

DON: It's from Melissa?

GUY: (*Not looking at him*) Yes ...

DON: (*Perturbed*) What is it, Guy?

GUY looks at DON and makes an effort to collect his thoughts.

GUY: Don, this afternoon the Inspector and I saw that doctor of yours – Swanley ...

DON: Well?

GUY: He told the Inspector that ... He said I accused Melissa of having an affair with someone.

DON: Is that true?

GUY: No, of course not! Melissa had friends of her own – a good many friends – but never, never at any time did I suggest that she'd been unfaithful to me. (*He stops, looks at the letter again*) But this letter, this seems to confirm what Swanley said ... I just don't understand ...

DON: What's in the letter? What does it say?

GUY: (*Reading*) "Darling Guy, I'm sorry about the row. It was always my hope that you would never find out about Peter Antrobus. I tried to keep it from you. Even now I don't know what made you suspicious, darling. Whatever it was – please forgive me for all the unhappiness I have caused you. Melissa."

DON: (*Puzzled by the name*) Peter Antrobus? Who's Peter Antrobus?

GUY: (*Shaking his head*) That's just it ... (*Bewildered*) I don't know ...

GUY stares at the letter.

CUT TO: A corner table in the saloon bar of a public house,
London. Night.

*FELIX and GUY are sitting at the table; half empty glasses in
front of them. FELIX looks uncomfortable and faintly ill-at-
ease. GUY is smoking a cigarette, watching FELIX, still
patiently waiting to hear the reason for the telephone call.*

FELIX: Are – are you sure you wouldn't like another
         drink?

GUY: I'm sure.

FELIX: Just – just a short one, old chap?

GUY: No, I won't thanks. But don't mind me – you
         carry on, Felix.

FELIX: (*Nervously; turning round, looking towards the
         bar*) I think perhaps I'll have a Scotch this time.
         No – no, I won't, I'll have the same again.

GUY: (*Feeling in his pocket*) I'll do this.

FELIX: (*Rising*) No, no, don't worry about that; don't
         worry about that, my old dear.

*FELIX leaves the table and goes over to the bar. GUY
watches him for a moment, then takes out his wallet, unfolds
the I.O.U. and places it on the table. FELIX returns with his
drink and sits down.*

FELIX: (*Raising his glass*) Cheers!

*GUY nods. FELIX is about to drink when he sees the I.O.U.
He stops dead – glass in hand, mouth wide open. GUY picks
up the I.O.U.*

GUY: Isn't this what you wanted to see me about? (*He
         looks at the piece of paper*) I.O.U. Three thousand
         pounds. Felix Hepburn.

FELIX: Where – where did you get that?

GUY: Melissa had it.

FELIX: Yes, I know. I gave it to her. (*He takes out his
         handkerchief*) My God, I've been worried about
         that. (*He mops his face*) Have I been worried! I

50

knew the ruddy thing would turn up sooner or later and I didn't want it to get into the wrong hands. I mean, if that damn fool of an Inspector thought that Melissa had lent me … Now don't get me wrong, Guy! Don't get me wrong – you'll get the money! It's just a question of time …

GUY: This isn't my I.O.U., Felix. You didn't give it to me.

FELIX: Yes, I know, but it's yours now, surely, old chap?

GUY: Why did Melissa lend you three thousand pounds?

FELIX: I don't know why. It's always been a complete mystery to me, and that's the truth. It happened about six months ago. I hit a bad patch on the stock market. You know how it is. Some ruddy know-all in the City gives you a red hot tip where are you … Anyway, I was down the pan, old boy – well and truly. Of course, I could have got the money from Paula, but you know Paula. I'd never have heard the last of it. Then one day I drove down to Folkestone to see if I could "touch" an old chum of mine. "Chum", you can say that again! On the way back my car conked out at a place called Elvingdale. I went into a café while they were repairing the thing and, lo and behold, there was Melissa.

GUY: Was she alone?

FELIX: Yes. I was feeling ruddy depressed by this time – on the floor, in fact – and I'm afraid it was pretty obvious. In the end I poured out the whole story.

GUY: And she offered to lend you the money?

FELIX: Yes – just like that. (*He snaps his fingers*) You could have bowled me over. I was flabbergasted. I didn't think either of you had that sort of money to spare.

GUY: (*Quietly*) And what exactly did you have to do,
            Felix?
FELIX: (*Puzzled*) Do?
GUY: Yes – what did you have to do for the three
            thousand pounds?
FELIX: Why, nothing! Nothing at all. Except keep my
            mouth shut – and I was delighted to do that
            anyway.

GUY looks at FELIX, then rises from the table.

GUY: Felix, have you heard of a man called Peter
            Antrobus?
FELIX: No, never. Should I have done?
GUY: (*Shaking his head*) It's not important. Here's your
            I.O.U., Felix. If I were you, in future I'd leave
            high finance to the financiers, they know a little
            more about it.
FELIX: (*Stunned; taking the I.O.U.*) ... Yes, I think you're
            right, my old dear.

CUT TO: The Front Door of GUY FOSTER's Flat.
Evening.
*GUY arrives from his meeting with FELIX. He takes out his
key and lets himself into the flat.*

CUT TO: The Living Room of GUY's Flat. Evening.
*GUY enters the room from the hall, having disposed of his hat
and coat. He crosses to the drinks table, mixes himself a
whisky and soda, and then turns towards the bedroom.*
*As the camera pans GUY towards the bedroom, we see the
toes of a pair of high-heeled shoes protruding beneath the
living room curtains. The wearer of the shoes was obviously
in the flat when GUY arrived and took immediate refuge
behind the curtains.*

GUY stops for a second, glass in hand, thoughtfully looking round the room – then he continues into the bedroom.

CUT TO: The Bedroom of GUY's Flat. Evening.
GUY enters the bedroom; puts down his drink, loosens his tie, then takes off his jacket. He sits on the bed and is about to remove his shoes when there is the unmistakable sound of the front door closing. GUY looks up, astonished. He rushes back into the living room.

CUT TO: The Living Room of GUY's Flat. Evening.
The room is empty, but the curtains are swaying slightly. GUY stares at the curtains, then crosses towards them. He stands for a moment, near the curtains, and looking in the direction of the hall and the front door. It is obvious that he now realises what has happened. He is turning away from the curtains when he notices a small lace handkerchief on the floor. GUY picks it up and examines it. We see the initial "M" embossed on the handkerchief.
Puzzled, GUY walks slowly back into the centre of the room. He looks at the initial "M" on the handkerchief, then across at the photograph of MELISSA, which is on the desk.   He moves towards the photograph.   The camera tracks towards the photograph of MELISSA.
GUY reaches out, about to pick up the photograph, then stops dead. He has noticed the typewriter. The cover has been removed, the position of the machine altered, and a sheet of paper inserted. GUY quickly stoops down and reads the typed message on the piece of paper which reads:
"You'll find Peter Antrobus at Elvingdale. Duncan's, Saturday morning, 10.30."

53

CUT TO: Elvingdale: an attractive village in Kent. Saturday morning.

The official car park is almost full when GUY arrives in his Hillman Minx. He parks the car, then joins the white-coated YOUTH who stands, mouth open, watching him.

GUY: How much do I owe you?

YOUTH: Tanner.

GUY gives the youth a two-shilling piece and waits for his change.

GUY: Is there a café here called Duncan's …?

YOUTH: Never heard of it. What d'you give me – two bob?

As the YOUTH searches in his satchel for change, GUY becomes interested in a Bentley, parked near a sign which reads "Elvingdale, Official Car Park".

GUY: (*His eyes on the car; quietly*) Yes.

The YOUTH gives GUY his change and strolls towards a newly arrived motorist.

GUY crosses towards the exit; as he reaches the pavement he turns and looks at the Bentley. The chauffeur is at the wheel, obviously waiting for someone. He recognises GUY and stares back at him, unsmiling. As GUY walks past the car, he glances down at the registration number – NS 100.

CUT TO: Elvingdale High Street; Saturday morning.

GUY is strolling down the pavement, looking at the various shops, when JOYCE DEAN emerges from a book shop on the opposite side of the road. GUY recognises her almost immediately; he watches her with interest as she proceeds down the High Street. It is obvious that she hasn't seen GUY and is blissfully unaware of being watched.

As GUY turns, from watching JOYCE DEAN, he notices a Gent's Hairdresser's on the other side of the road. The sign over the window reads: DUNCAN's; there is a small barber's pole attached to the door of the shop. GUY crosses, and looks in the shop window.

CUT TO: DUNCAN's: a small barber's shop in Elvingdale. Saturday morning.

The room is tidy, clear, and gaily decorated with numerous advertisements for razor blades, hair tonics, lotions, etc. There is a showcase complete with electric razors, combs, brushes, and tubes of shaving cream. A long, padded bench stands near the door and there are two revolving chairs in the centre of the room facing mirrors and wash basins.

DUNCAN – a neat, spruce looking man – sits in one of the chairs reading a newspaper. His assistant – JACKSON – is busy tidying up.

The door opens and GUY enters from the street. DUNCAN immediately puts down the newspaper and jumps out of the chair.

DUNCAN: Good morning, sir.

GUY: Good morning. Er – is it possible to have a haircut?

DUNCAN: Yes, certainly, sir. Jackson …

JACKSON turns away from the basin he is cleaning and indicates his chair. GUY climbs into the chair, glancing up at the clock on the wall as he does so. It is 10.32.

JACKSON moves back to the basin, finally collecting his bits and pieces before attending to GUY.

The door opens and TOM BILLINGS enters; he is a local farmer. GUY quickly looks towards the door.

BILLINGS: (*To DUNCAN*) Are you free?

DUNCAN: Sorry, Mr Billings. I've got an appointment.

BILLINGS: (*Annoyed*) Always the same on a Saturday morning.

DUNCAN: If you'd been two minutes earlier.

BILLINGS: Yes, I know. I've heard that one before. What time's your appointment?

DUNCAN: Ten-thirty. (*Glancing at the clock*) He's late.

BILLINGS: (*With sarcasm*) Mr Antrobus, I presume?

DUNCAN: Yes. I'll be through before eleven.

BILLINGS: Okay, I'll see you then.

He gives DUNCAN a nod and goes out.

JACKSON dries his hands, puts a "gown" over GUY, and begins to sort out his combs, scissors, etc.

JACKSON: Very mild for the time of the year.

GUY: (*His eyes still on the door*) Yes – yes, it is.

JACKSON moves behind the chair.

JACKSON: How would you like it?

GUY: (*Taking his eyes off the door for the first time*) Oh – just a trim, please. Don't take too much off.

JACKSON: That makes a nice change.

The door opens to admit another customer and GUY quickly turns his head.

The camera pans to show a good-looking BOY of about twelve standing in the doorway; a school cap on the back of his head.

DUNCAN: (*With a faintly reprimanding air*) Good morning, Mr Antrobus.

PETER: Sorry if I'm late.

DUNCAN smiles and indicates his chair.

DUNCAN: Come along, Peter.

The BOY climbs into the chair, then turns and looks at GUY who is staring at him in astonishment.

END OF EPISODE TWO

EPISODE THREE

OPEN TO: DUNCAN's: a small barber's shop in Elvingdale. Saturday morning.

GUY has now had his haircut and he is slowly getting out of the chair, wiping the nape of his neck with a hand towel.

DUNCAN has completed his work on PETER ANTROBUS and the boy is going through more or less the same routine as GUY. GUY looks across at the boy and gives a friendly nod.

GUY: Hate having my hair cut, don't you? I think I'd sooner go to the dentist.

The BOY smiles.

DUNCAN: (*To PETER*) I'll bet <u>you</u> wouldn't.

GUY: (*To PETER; feeling his collar*) I don't know why it is, but the hairs always get down my neck. Never fails. (*To JACKSON*) How much do I owe you?

JACKSON: Three bob, please, sir.

GUY: (*Turning; to PETER*) Elvingdale seems a nice place. Do you live down here?

PETER: Yes, sir. Well – just outside.

DUNCAN: First time you've been to Elvingdale?

GUY: Yes, it is.

JACKSON: Funny, I thought I'd seen you before, sir.

GUY: (*Shaking his head*) I know Calford fairly well and Lenton-on-Sea.

JACKSON: Now that's a pretty little place!

GUY: Yes, I've got a cottage near Lenton.

DUNCAN: What is Lenton – about seventeen miles from here?

JACKSON: (*Shaking his head*) It's more than that. (*Using a clothes-brush on GUY*) Must be all of twenty-four or five.

DUNCAN: Never!

JACKSON: It is, you know.

PETER: It's fifteen miles from our place.

59

JACKSON:	Only fifteen? Are you sure?
PETER:	Yes, I'm positive, Mr Jackson. There's a sign just past our garage.

MARY ANTROBUS bursts into the shop. She is in her early twenties; a tense, nervous looking girl. She wears jeans and is carrying a mass of parcels.

MARY:	For heaven's sake, Peter – get a move on! We haven't got all morning!
DUNCAN:	(*Grinning*) Good morning, Miss Antrobus.
MARY:	Hello, Mr Duncan! (*Trying to find her handbag*) How much do we owe you?
DUNCAN:	Oh, don't worry about that, Miss. I'll charge it.
MARY:	(*To PETER*) You know what Father said – we've got to be back by half past eleven!
PETER:	(*Irritated; picking up his cap*) Don't fuss, Mary! We've got bags of time.
MARY:	We haven't got bags of time! It's all right for you, you're on holiday!
GUY:	(*To MARY; pleasantly*) I'm afraid it's my fault, I kept your brother talking.
MARY:	(*Smiling*) Oh, that's all right, but I know what Peter is. Once he starts nattering you can never ... stop ... him ... (*The smile has faded; she has recognised GUY*)

JACKSON stares at MARY, puzzled, then at GUY.

MARY:	Come on, Peter.

PETER joins MARY.

PETER:	Bye, Mr Duncan.
DUNCAN:	Goodbye, Peter. Goodbye, Miss Antrobus. Remember me to your father.

MARY nods, ushers PETER out of the shop, and, after a quick glance at GUY, follows him.

GUY: (*To JACKSON; a shade embarrassed*) How
               much did you say?
JACKSON: (*Studying GUY*) Three shillings.
GUY: Thank you. (*He gives JACKSON four shillings*)
               Keep the change.
*JACKSON nods and puts the money in his pocket. GUY picks
up his hat, hesitates, as if about to say something, then
changes his mind.*
GUY: Good morning.
JACKSON: Good morning, sir.
DUNCAN: (*Quietly*) Good morning, sir – thank you.
GUY goes out.
DUNCAN: (*Quickly; as the door closes*) Who is that
               chap?
JACKSON: (*Excited; faintly pleased with himself*) Don't
               you know? Miss Antrobus recognised him.
DUNCAN: Yes, I could see that. But who is he?
*JACKSON turns, crosses to the bench, and picks up a
newspaper. He searches the paper, finds what he wants, and
returns to DUNCAN.*
JACKSON: (*Holding out the paper*) There he is …
*We see the newspaper in JACKSON's hand. We see two
photographs; one of MELISSA and the other of GUY. The
caption reads: "Who murdered MELISSA FOSTER?"
JACKSON lowers the newspaper and looks towards the door.*

CUT TO: The High Street, Elvingdale. Saturday morning.
*GUY is walking down the street, returning to the car park.
He is deep in thought, turning over in his mind the incident
with MARY ANTROBUS.*
*JOYCE DEAN emerges from a shop and almost bumps into
him.*
JOYCE: I beg your pardon …
GUY: I'm sorry, I …

GUY and JOYCE recognise each other.

JOYCE: (*Without thinking*) Oh, I'm sorry, Mr Foster, I didn't recognise you.

GUY: (*With the suggestion of a smile*) You recognised me the last time we met. You made quite a point of it. (*Taking hold of JOYCE's arm*) No, don't go, Miss Dean, please! Is Dr Swanley with you?

JOYCE: No, I'm visiting my mother; she lives in Elvingdale.

GUY: Oh, I see. (*He releases JOYCE's arm*) Miss Dean, why did you tell Inspector Carter that we'd met before?

JOYCE: (*Puzzled*) Why? Because he asked me if I'd ever seen you before – that's why.

GUY: You told him that I'd consulted Dr Swanley. You said you – yourself – showed me into the consulting room?

JOYCE: That's right.

GUY: (*Shaking his head*) But that isn't true! You know perfectly well it isn't true!

DR SWANLEY's car drives up to the kerb. The CHAUFFEUR looks at GUY and JOYCE DEAN, then leaning across the car opens the passenger door.

JOYCE: Mr Foster, you've gone through a great deal just recently and I feel sorry for you, very sorry. But when I'm asked a perfectly straightforward question by someone …

GUY: (*Angrily*) I don't want you to feel sorry for me! I just want you to tell the truth.

JOYCE: (*Facing GUY; quite simply*) But I've told the truth! Now, if you'll excuse me …

GUY: (*Relenting*) Miss Dean, please! Wait – just a second …

JOYCE: (*Hesitating*) Well – what is it?

GUY: I apologise. I shouldn't have lost my temper like
            that. I'm sorry.
JOYCE: (*Pleasantly*) It's all right, Mr Foster, I understand
            …
GUY: You think I'm lying about all this, don't you?
JOYCE: (*After a moment; shaking her head*) No, I don't
            think you're lying, not deliberately. I just think
            you've been ill and this business with your wife
            has been too much for you.
GUY: You mean – it's affected my memory, is that it?
*JOYCE looks at GUY; it would appear she is a little sorry for
him.*
GUY: Well – is that what you think?
JOYCE: (*Quietly; with a little nod*) Yes. But remember,
            I'm not a doctor, Mr Foster, or a police inspector –
            I'm just a secretary.
JOYCE turns and gets into the car.

CUT TO: The Car Park. Elvingdale. Day.
*GUY has reached the car park and is walking, deep in
thought, towards his car. He suddenly realises that he is
approaching PETER and MARY ANTROBUS who are
standing by a shooting brake. The girl – still precariously
loaded with parcels – is searching her handbag for the car
key. As GUY draws level, she drops several of her parcels and
he immediately springs forwards and retrieves them for her.*
*GUY returns the parcels to the embarrassed MARY, smiles at
her brother, and continues towards the Hillman.*
*GUY reaches his car, unlocks it, and gets inside. He is
reversing the car when an elderly ATTENDANT appears on
the scene and starts to issue instructions.*
*MARY ANTROBUS drives past in the shooting brake and the
ATTENDANT turns and waves to her. She waves back;
ignoring GUY.*

GUY winds down the car window and gives the man an unexpected tip.

ATTENDANT: (*Surprised*) Oh, thank you, sir.

GUY: Was that Miss Harris you just waved to?

ATTENDANT: Harris? No, sir – that was Miss Antrobus.

GUY: Oh, I'm sorry. Antrobus? That's an unusual name. Is it fairly common in these parts?

ATTENDANT: No, I don't think so. There's only the one family, so far as I know. Her father runs that garage – the big one just before you get into the village.

GUY: (*Casually*) I think I've seen him – tallish chap, wears glasses, about forty-five ...

ATTENDANT: (*Shaking his head*) No, no, that's not George Antrobus. George must be fifty-five if he's a day. Looks older, too, sometimes, poor devil.

GUY: Why poor devil?

ATTENDANT: Oh, he's had a basinful just lately. Lost his wife about eighteen months ago – rushed into hospital himself just before Christmas. (*He notices a new arrival*) Well – thank you, sir.

GUY nods and closes the car window.

CUT TO: GEORGE ANTROBUS's Garage near Elvingdale. Afternoon.

This is a large garage with showrooms, drive-in for petrol, a service station, etc. There is an office attached to the showroom. The camera pans to reveal the name GEORGE ANTROBUS prominently displayed over the entrance to the garage.

GUY is standing near his car, waiting to be served with petrol. MARY ANTROBUS comes out of the showroom and goes into the office. GUY watches her for a moment, then throwing away his cigarette, crosses towards the office.

CUT TO: The Garage Office. Afternoon.

It is a pleasant, roomy office, very well stocked with car accessories. There is a desk, two chairs, and a filing cabinet. There is a signed photograph of DON PAGE on the desk, obviously taken at a Grand Prix. DON can be seen leaning against a Ferrari, smiling, helmet and goggles in hand.

MARY ANTROBUS is standing behind the desk, reading a letter, when GUY enters.

GUY: Miss Antrobus, may I have a word with you?

MARY: (*Nervously*) What is it you want?

MARY puts the letter down on the desk. GUY is now staring at the photograph of DON PAGE.

MARY: (*Impatiently*) Well – what is it?

GUY: (*Suddenly*) Oh, I beg your pardon ... My name's Foster – Guy Foster ...

MARY: Yes, I know, I recognised you this morning. I've seen your photograph in the papers.

GUY nods.

MARY: You're the man who murd – whose wife was murdered.

GUY: (*He nods*) Yes, and because of that I'm trying to find out certain things about my wife. I think perhaps you might be able to help me.

MARY: How can I help you?

GUY: Melissa – my wife – was friendly with someone called Peter Antrobus and I was wondering ...

MARY: (*Surprised*) Peter Antrobus? (*Amused*) Why, that's my brother! He's still at school ... You spoke to him, in Duncan's ...

65

GUY: Yes, I know, and that's why I want to talk to you. Have you a relative in Elvingdale, or do you happen to know anyone, with the same name as your brother?

MARY: No, I'm afraid I don't.

GUY: (*Looking at MARY*) You're sure?

MARY: Of course I'm sure! I don't even know anyone else called Antrobus – apart from my father of course. (*Curious*) But what makes you think your wife was friendly with a man called Peter Antrobus?

GUY: She left me a letter. The name was mentioned in it.

MARY: I see. Well, I'm sorry, Mr Foster, I can't help you. I never met your wife, and I'm quite sure Peter didn't.

GUY: And you've never heard of anyone with the same name as your brother?

MARY: No, I've already told you that.

MARY picks up the letter and looks at it. GUY turns towards the door, then hesitates.

GUY: This morning, after I left Duncan's, I bumped into a woman called Joyce Dean.

MARY looks up.

GUY: Apparently she used to live down here – her mother still does.

MARY: Well?

GUY: I was wondering if you knew her.

MARY: Why should I know her?

GUY: No reason at all, but Elvingdale's a fairly small place and – (*A shrug*) I just wondered if you did.

MARY: Is she a friend of yours?

GUY: No, not exactly.

MARY: Then why are you interested in her?

66

GUY: She made a statement to the police – a false statement, I'm afraid.

MARY: About your wife?

GUY: No – about me.

MARY looks at GUY; she almost seems to be making her mind up about something.

MARY: What did you say her name was? Joyce –?

GUY: Dean. She's a nurse. Well, secretary-cum-nurse.

MARY: Funnily enough, I do know her. At least, I've met her. Don't know anything about her, though ... She used to work in the local hospital. I think she left here about a year ago.

GUY: She now works for a man called Swanley.

MARY: Swanley? (*She shakes her head*) Never heard of him.

GUY: He's a doctor.

MARY: In London?

GUY: Yes – in Wimpole Street.

MARY: Some people have all the luck! Wish to goodness I worked in London!

GUY: You probably wouldn't like it if you did – especially in the summer.

MARY: What summer?

GUY smiles. MARY becomes interested in her letter again.

GUY: (*After a moment*) Well – thank you, Miss Antrobus.

MARY: Sorry I can't help you.

GUY: At least you've tried.

MARY looks up, not quite sure how to take this remark. GUY goes out.

CUT TO: The Front Door of DON PAGE's Flat in St John's Wood. Evening.

GUY is standing at the door, his finger on the bell push; from inside the flat we can hear musical chimes. The door is opened by DON, resplendent in a new smoking jacket – he is obviously expecting someone but is very surprised to find that his visitor is GUY.

DON: Why, hello, Guy.

GUY: Have I interrupted your dinner?

DON: No, I … I'm expecting friends.

GUY: May I come in?

DON: Yes – yes, of course, old boy.

GUY enters the flat.

CUT TO: The Drawing Room of Don's Flat. Evening.

A large, ornate table has been prepared with drinks, canapes, etc. GUY enters, followed by DON.

DON: Let me get you a drink.

GUY: Could I have a Scotch?

DON: Yes, certainly.

GUY: (*Looking at the table*) Are you giving a party?

DON: No – no, hardly a party, old boy. Just expecting a few friends. (*At the table*) Soda?

GUY: Thank you. (*As Don mixes the drink*) I've just returned from a place called Elvingdale. Do you know it?

DON: It's in Kent?

GUY: Yes.

DON: I've driven through it once or twice, never actually stopped there.

GUY: Someone broke into my flat and left a note for me. The note said I'd find Peter Antrobus at Elvingdale – that's why I went down there.

DON: (*Turning; curious*) Peter Antrobus – the man Melissa mentioned?

GUY: That's right.

DON: Was he in Elvingdale?

GUY: (*Shaking his head*) No. Well – there was a Peter Antrobus there, but I doubt very much whether he was a friend of Melissa's. He's twelve years old and still at school.

DON: Maybe it's his father you should be interested in; perhaps he's called Peter too?

GUY: No, his name's George. George Antrobus. He's a widower; man of about fifty-five; owns a garage. I thought you might have met him, Don?

DON: Why do you say that?

GUY: They've got a signed photograph of you in the office.

DON: Oh, I see.

GUY: Mary – the daughter – seems a strange girl, but quite attractive. (*Looking at DON*) About twenty-two or three, I suppose.

DON: I'm afraid I haven't met either of them.

DON turns from the table and offers GUY the whisky and soda.

GUY: No? (*Taking the drink*) Well, I wondered, that's all.

DON: Because of the photograph?

GUY: Yes.

DON: (*A shrug*) I've signed hundreds of those things, old boy – they're all over the place. (*Raising his glass*) Cheers! (*He drinks then puts his glass down on the table*) Guy, I'm glad you dropped in tonight, because there's something I want to ask you. You know that I.O.U.; the one you found in the deedbox?

The front door chimes can be heard.

GUY: Yes.

DON: I know it's none of my business and I shouldn't really ask this question, but ... Was it Felix?

GUY: What do you mean?

DON: The I.O.U. – was it signed by Felix?

GUY: (*Nodding towards the hall*) I think your friends have arrived, Don.

DON hesitates, looks at GUY – not sure whether he is evading the question or not – and goes out into the hall.

After a moment GUY hears the front door open and the sound of voices.

PAULA: (*Off*) My God, just look at that jacket, Felix! Where on earth did you dig that up?

FELIX: (*Off*) Sorry we're late, Don, but Paula would drag me along to ... (*Realising that DON is talking to PAULA, confidentially*) What's that, my old dear?

GUY cannot hear what DON is saying and a few seconds later they all enter the drawing room.

PAULA: Hello, Guy! How are you sweetie?

GUY: Hello, Paula! Felix ...

FELIX: Nice to see you, Guy. You look better – much better, doesn't he, Paula?

PAULA: Guy, Felix and I were talking about you this morning and we were wondering if you'd like to come away with us for the weekend? We could drive down to the coast or even ...

GUY: No, thank you, Paula. It's very kind of you both and I appreciate it, but I'm thinking of going down to the cottage for three or four weeks. I've still got quite a lot of work to do on my book and I don't seem to be able to get on with it in Town.

FELIX: I'm not surprised, old man.

DON: (*At the drinks table*) Have you still got that cottage, Guy? I thought you'd got rid of it?

GUY: No, we put it up for sale about a year ago but nothing happened.

PAULA: I could never understand why you didn't spend more time down there, you always said you liked Lenton.

GUY: Yes, but unfortunately Melissa hated it. In the end I couldn't even get her down for weekends.

DON: (*To PAULA*) Gin and tonic?

PAULA: Thank you, Duckie.

FELIX: Scotch for me, old boy. (*To GUY*) If I were in your shoes, I'd certainly move down to Lenton, if only to get away from that Carter character. My God, he's a persistent type if you like!

DON: (*Only half listening to FELIX*) Who's that, Felix?

FELIX: Carter – the Scotland Yard chap. Do you know the confounded fellow spent almost an hour with us this morning?

PAULA: Don't exaggerate, Felix.

FELIX: Forty minutes, anyway, old girl.

GUY: I wasn't mentioned, by any chance?

PAULA: Funnily enough, you weren't, Guy – at least, only indirectly. It was old Don he seemed to be principally interested in.

DON: (*Turning*) Me?

FELIX: Yes.

DON: Why me?

FELIX: Well – it was all mixed up with what he called the time element, old boy. How long it took you to take Carol home. What time we dropped Melissa …

GUY: (*Interrupting FELIX; curious*) Carol? Carol who?

DON: Carol Stewart was at the party. She got tiddly as usual and insisted on doing that corny old act of

71

hers. In the end she was such a confounded nuisance I had to take her home.

PAULA: Actually, the poor darling was frightfully sick …

FELIX: But she's always sick, Paula – she makes a thing of it! (*To GUY*) First of all she drinks too much, then she does that terrible act, and finally she insists on the host – must be the host, old man – driving her home. (*To DON*) Felt sorry for you, my old dear, having to dash off like that.

DON: It was my fault, I asked for it. I should never have invited her in the first place. (*Handing drinks to PAULA and FELIX*) But I still don't see why Carter was interested in me.

GUY: We know that Melissa left Paula and Felix at about eight-fifteen. Where she went after that, or what happened, we don't know. It was approx.-imately three hours later that they found her in Regent's Park.

DON: (*Puzzled*) So?

GUY: So obviously she was murdered between eight-fifteen and half past eleven.

DON: Yes, I can see that, but it still doesn't explain why Carter should be curious about me. After all, I was here all night; the party started at eight and didn't finish until after midnight.

GUY: Were you here all night, Don?

DON: Yes, of course I was; except for the time when Carol … (*He stops; looks at GUY, then at FELIX*) My God, now I get the point! Now I see what the Inspector was getting at! A chap throws a party and suddenly disappears in the middle of it. Paula, I hope to God you told him about Carol – I hope you explained exactly what happened?

72

PAULA: Don't worry, Don – we told him. We explained the whole situation, didn't we, Felix?

FELIX: Yes, of course. In any case, it's a hundred to one he'll have a word with Carol anyway.

In spite of what FELIX says DON looks distinctly worried.

GUY: How long were you away, Don?

DON: (*Surprised by the question*) From the flat?

GUY: Yes.

DON: About twenty-five minutes, I suppose. Half an hour at the outside. Carol has a flat near Baker Street. I simply dumped her on the doorstep – didn't even bother to go inside.

FELIX: I'll bet you were invited?

DON: Yes, I was invited all right.

FELIX: (*To PAULA*) Of course you were. (*To DON*) That's what she was after, you know – that's what she really wanted, old boy. You whooping it up with her while the party went for a Burton.

PAULA: (*Laughing*) I think you're very unkind, Felix.

FELIX: It's true, my old dear, and you know it.

FELIX moves to the table and helps himself to canapes.

GUY: Was Melissa a friend of hers?

PAULA: Yes, they were quite good friends. I'm surprised you never met her, Guy.

GUY: I think I did meet her once, about a year ago. We went to a cocktail party, and she turned up very late with a Siamese cat.

FELIX: That's our Carol!

The front door chimes can be heard.

DON: (*Moving towards FELIX*) Felix, did this detective – what's-his-name, Carter? – ask you anything else about me?

FELIX: No – only what we've told you, old boy.

PAULA: Now for heaven's sake don't you get the wrong impression, Don! He was only interested in you because you left the party for a little while, that's all. (*To FELIX*) After all, he asked you enough questions about that phone call ...

FELIX: Ye gods, he certainly did!

GUY: Which phone call was that?

FELIX: (*Eating canapes*) The one I made to you, old boy, and couldn't get through.

GUY: I don't know why you didn't get through, Felix, I was in the flat all evening.

BAKER, a manservant, comes out of the dining room and crosses into the hall.

FELIX: (*Helping himself to more canapes*) Perhaps the phone was out of order. Don's was ...

GUY: No, the phone was all right because Melissa telephoned.

FELIX: I probably dialled the wrong number; it was frightfully difficult to see anyway. (*To DON; indicating the canapes*) I say, these are jolly tasty, Don.

GUY: (*Puzzled*) What do you mean, Felix – it was difficult to see? Didn't you phone from here?

FELIX: No, I've just told you, Don's phone was out of order. I popped out to a box.

DON: That must have been while I was taking Carol home?

FELIX: Yes, it was, old boy.

FELIX realises that GUY is looking at him.

FELIX: There's no mystery about this phone call, my old dear. If you were in the flat and the phone didn't ring, then obviously I dialled the wrong number.

GUY: Did you tell Carter you didn't phone from here?

FELIX: Tell him! Good God, what do you think he was
            questioning me about? I even had to describe the
            ruddy phone box. Didn't I, Paula?

Voices can be heard in the hall.

DON: Excuse me ...

*DON moves across to the hall as BAKER returns with
CAROL STEWART who is an attractively dressed woman in
her late forties.*

BAKER: Miss Stewart, sir.

DON: (*Surprised*) Hello, Carol!

BAKER returns to the dining room.

CAROL: Don, I'm sorry if I've interrupted a party but –
            (*She stops; looks at GUY*)

DON: I'm delighted to see you, Carol. You know Paula,
            of course, and Felix?

CAROL: Yes, of course.

PAULA: Hello, Duckie – are you feeling any better?

CAROL: Yes – yes, I'm fine now, thank you.

FELIX: Nice to see you again, Carol.

DON: This is Guy Foster. I think you have met, once
            before ...

CAROL: (*Not quite sure what to say*) Yes ... How are you,
            Mr Foster? I – I was terribly shocked when I heard
            about ... Melissa ...

FELIX: (*Mumbling*) My God, yes ...

PAULA: I think we all were, Carol.

CAROL: (*To GUY*) Have the police any idea who did it?

GUY: I don't honestly know. It's difficult to tell whether
            they have any information or not. A man called
            Carter is in charge of the case. He seems very
            efficient ...

CAROL: Yes, I've met him. He came to see me this
            morning.

75

PAULA: I expect he asked you a lot of pointless questions, Duckie?

CAROL: (*Looking at PAULA; quietly*) He asked a lot of questions, certainly.

FELIX: I'll bet he wanted to know how long old Don was with you the other night? How long it took him to get you home?

CAROL: (*Still looking at FELIX*) Yes – amongst other things.

DON: What do you mean, Carol – amongst other things?

CAROL: (*Turning towards him*) Well, obviously he asked me about Melissa. How long I'd known her; whether we were good friends or not.

DON: Oh – Oh, I see.

An uncomfortable pause.

DON: (*Suddenly*) Carol, let me get you a drink?

CAROL: No, I won't, Don, thank you. I'm going to the theatre, and I've got someone waiting for me downstairs. It was just that ... (*Searching for an excuse for the visit*) It was just that I wanted to have a word with you, that's all. I'll give you a ring tomorrow, Don.

DON: (*Curious*) Yes, all right, Carol.

CAROL: (*To PAULA; having thought of an excuse*) I'm organising a charity "do" and I'd like Don to help us out, if he would. (*To DON*) But don't worry, darling, I'll phone you tomorrow and tell you all about it – you can wriggle out of it then.

DON laughs.

CAROL: Goodbye, Felix. Paula ...

FELIX: Goodbye, Carol.

CAROL smiles at GUY and turns towards the hall.

DON: I'll come down with you, Carol. (*To the others*) Help yourself to drinks, everyone.

76

CAROL and DON go out into the hall.

CUT TO: The Corridor outside of DON's front door. Night.
The door opens and CAROL enters the corridor followed by DON. DON quickly closes the door behind him and, taking hold of CAROL's arm, draws her towards him; he talks quietly, confidentially.

DON: Carol, what happened this morning? What else did the Inspector say to you?

CAROL: (*Quickly*) That's what I wanted to talk to you about – that's why I came here.

DON: Yes, I realise that. I only hope to goodness you told him the truth, Carol?

CAROL: (*Resentfully*) Of course I told him the truth! Whatever do you mean?

DON: I'm sorry, but apparently he also questioned Felix about me. He wanted to know how long I was away from the flat and what exactly happened.

CAROL: (*Surprised*) He questioned <u>Felix</u> about <u>you</u>?

DON: Yes; and I can understand why. After all, it was my party so you'd hardly expect me to … *(He looks at CAROL)* But you sound surprised?

CAROL: I am surprised.

DON: Why?

CAROL: Because he questioned <u>me</u> about Felix. (*Shaking her head*) He wasn't a bit interested in you, Don.

DON stares at CAROL.

DON: He questioned <u>you</u> about <u>Felix</u>?

CAROL: (*She nods towards the door of the flat*) Yes, that's why I was so embarrassed when I found that Felix was here.

DON: What exactly did the Inspector ask you about Felix?

77

CAROL: He wanted to know if he'd ever tried to borrow money from me.

DON: What did you say?

CAROL: I told him he had. He tried to borrow five hundred pounds from me about a year ago. Unsuccessfully, I might add.

DON: Go on, Carol. Did he ask you anything else?

CAROL: Yes, he asked me whether Felix had made a phone call while he was at the party. I said I wasn't sure, but I didn't think he had.

DON: (*His thoughts elsewhere*) He made one later, from a callbox. It was while I was taking you home; my phone was out of order.

CAROL: Who told you that?

DON looks at CAROL.

CAROL: It couldn't have been out of order for very long.

DON: (*Puzzled*) No?

CAROL: (*Shaking her head*) After you dropped me, I felt a little guilty, rather ashamed of myself, I'm afraid. I suddenly realised I'd behaved rather badly and probably spoilt the whole evening for you. Anyway, I phoned you, darling – just to apologise. Some woman or other answered the phone, I don't know who it was. I could hear the party going on in the background. (*A shrug*) You hadn't returned so I rang off.

DON: (*Puzzled*) But you got through all right?

CAROL: Yes, I had no difficulty at all.

DON is thoughtful for a moment.

DON: Did you tell the Inspector about your phone call?

CAROL: No, there was no point. It hadn't anything to do with Felix and that's all he seemed interested in. Don, I must fly, or I shall be late.

DON: Yes, all right, Carol. I'll give you a ring some time tomorrow.

DON kisses CAROL on the cheek.

CUT TO: The Drawing Room of DON's Flat. Night.
FELIX is mixing himself another drink.

FELIX: (*To GUY*) Are you sure you won't have another one, old man?

GUY: Yes, I'm sure, Felix … (*He looks at his watch*)

DON comes in from the hall; he still looks thoughtful.

PAULA: We thought you'd got lost, Don. What have you been doing, telling her the story of your life?

DON: You know Carol, once she gets started. (*Changing the subject*) Guy, you'll stop and have some dinner with us?

GUY: Thank you, Don – but if you don't mind, I'd rather not …

DON: Really, old boy?

FELIX: (*To GUY*) Come along, my old dear.

GUY: Not tonight, if you don't mind, Don.

DON: Well, have another drink anyway – just for the road.

GUY: (*He hesitates, then:*) All right – I'll have a brandy and ginger ale this time.

FELIX: (*At the table*) One brandy and ginger ale – coming up!

DON looks across at FELIX.

CUT TO: The Living Room of GUY's Flat. Evening.
GUY enters; he carries his hat and overcoat and an evening newspaper. He takes off his things, throws them down on the settee, and opens the newspaper. There is a photograph of GUY and MELISSA on the front page, obviously taken on holiday several years ago.

GUY tosses the paper aside and crosses to the drinks table. He pours himself a large whisky, reaches for the soda, then changing his mind drinks it neat. He pours himself another whisky, picks up the decanter and moves to the armchair near the desk. He puts the decanter on the corner of the desk, loosens his tie and collar, and drops into the chair.

CUT TO: The Living Room of GUY's Flat. An hour later.
The decanter on the corner of the desk is now only a third full. The camera pans to show GUY half slumped in the armchair, glass in hand. His coat is off, shirt undone; a half open book on the arm of the chair.
After a moment he rises, crosses to the decanter, and pours himself another whisky. He drinks, replenishes his glass, and moves back to the chair. He stands by the chair, deep in thought, seemingly staring down at the book.
The phone rings.
GUY quickly turns and looks towards the desk. The phone continues ringing. Suddenly, tense and exasperated, he picks up the book and hurls it at the desk. The phone goes on ringing. Angry at his failure to silence the phone he lurches across the room and snatches up the receiver.
GUY: (*On the phone*) Hello? … Who do you want? …
           (*Silence*) Hello? …
We hear a woman's voice on the other end; it could well be the voice of MELISSA FOSTER – the same tone; the same inflections. She sounds strained; overwrought.
VOICE: Is that you, Guy?
GUY: What? (*Confused*) Who is that?
VOICE: Guy, this is Melissa …
GUY: (*Stunned*) Melissa …?
VOICE: Yes, darling. Now listen … I've got to see you, it's important – but you mustn't say anything to anyone about this, you understand?

GUY:	Melissa, where are you? Where the hell are you?
VOICE:	(*Tensely; apparently frightened*) Guy, did you hear what I said?
GUY:	Yes, I heard but ... Melissa, where are you? Where are you speaking from?
VOICE:	I'm at the cottage, at Lenton ... Get down here as soon as you can. (*Softly; near to tears*) Please, Guy – please ... (*She rings off*)

GUY replaces the receiver and slowly turns from the desk.

CUT TO: A Mews near GUY FOSTER's Flat. Night.
GUY drives his car out of a private lock-up garage. The Hillman stalls and GUY can be seen through the windscreen of the car impatiently pressing the starting button. Finally, the engine fires again and the car, being in gear, lurches forward. It is obvious that GUY is unfit to drive.

CUT TO: A Country Lane. Night.
The lane is deserted – then GUY's car suddenly appears in the distance. The Hillman is being driven far too fast – it skids, almost overturns into a ditch, then more by luck than judgement manages to right itself. The car continues down the lane.

CUT TO: A Main Road. Country. Night.
GUY is at the driving wheel of his car. The alcohol is now having its effect on him. He looks tired, hardly able to keep awake. Suddenly an approaching car races past, the lights momentarily blinding GUY and lighting up the interior of the Hillman. With a start, GUY pulls himself together and makes a determined effort to concentrate.
GUY miraculously pulls himself together again, just in time to avoid driving the Hillman into a group of trees by the side of

the road. He glances at his watch; realising now that he cannot continue like this.

Suddenly a grass bank can be seen about fifty yards past the trees and GUY, making a quick decision, drives the car off the road and onto the bank. As the car brakes to a standstill, he slumps forward over the driving wheel.

CUT TO: A Country Road. Several hours later.

A lorry is being driven along the road. The driver, HARRY KIRKLAND, is whistling to himself – suddenly, ahead of him, he notices GUY's car parked at a strange angle facing the bank. He drives past the Hillman – then seeing GUY slumped over the wheel, he pulls the lorry into the side of the road and climbs out.

CUT TO: Inside the Hilman.

GUY is asleep. HARRY arrives and peers at him through the partly open car window. GUY stirs; moves away from the wheel; glances up and sees HARRY peering at him.

HARRY: Are you okay?

GUY: Yes, I – I think so. I've been asleep. What time is it?

HARRY: About four o'clock. (*Grinning as he turns away*) Sorry if I've spoilt your kip, mate.

GUY slowly comes back to life; he is obviously suffering from a colossal hangover. He hears the noise of the lorry starting up in the background and winces with pain as he turns his head to look at it. He takes out a packet of cigarettes and lights one; then, after a quick glance at his watch, starts the car.

CUT TO: A cul-de-sac lane near Sand Dunes at Lenton-on-Sea. Early Morning.

There is a single lonely cottage at the end of the lane with the name "The Dunes" displayed on a rickety gate. The lights are on in the cottage.

GUY's car turns into the lane and pulls up outside the gate. GUY jumps out of the car and, running up the drive, unlocks the front door and lets himself into the cottage.

CUT TO: The Hall of The Dunes. Early Morning.

This is a pleasant but sparsely furnished room; there is a hallstand and a corner table with drawers and a telephone.

GUY enters the hall and closes the front door; as he turns and looks towards the living room he calls softly: "Melissa!"

Suddenly he stops, having obviously seen something on the floor near the table. The camera pans down to show a pair of gloves, suitable for gardening.

GUY slowly picks up the gloves and looks at them – as he does so he notices that the kitchen door at the far end of the room is partly open and the light is on.

The camera tracks in towards the kitchen. A woman's hand and part of her arm can be seen on the floor, protruding beyond the partly open door.

GUY suddenly rushes into picture, quickly pushing open the kitchen door. We see the dead body of MARY ANTROBUS.

GUY stares down at her; horrified – still holding the gloves in his hand.

END OF EPISODE THREE

EPISODE FOUR

OPEN TO: The Hall of The Dunes. Early Morning.

GUY is standing by the open kitchen door staring down at the body of MARY ANTROBUS – he is still holding the gloves in his hand. After a little while he kneels down, as if to examine the dead girl. Then suddenly, he thinks better of it and moves back to the table in the hall. He picks up the phone and starts to dial: his hands visibly trembling.

CUT TO: The Living Room of The Dunes. Early Morning.

The room is simply and inexpensively furnished: several chintz covered chairs: a worn but comfortable looking settee.

GUY is sitting on the settee talking to a member of the local C.I.D. – DETECTIVE SERGEANT HESTON. Through the open door we can see the hall where a police doctor, photographer, and several uniformed men appear to be in conference. HESTON, a self-possessed man of about forty, is studying his notebook.

GUY: (*Tensely: on edge*) I don't want to be difficult, Sergeant, but will you please get in touch with Inspector Carter?

HESTON: (*Looking up*) Yes, I'll get in touch with the Inspector, Mr Foster. All in good time.

HESTON consults his notebook again.

HESTON: Now, sir – you admit that you knew the young lady?

GUY: Yes, I've already told you that.

HESTON: She was in fact a friend of yours?

GUY rises.

GUY: She was <u>not</u> a friend of mine! I thought I'd made that quite clear?

HESTON: If you'll forgive my saying so, sir, you haven't made anything very clear. You've told me that the cottage belongs to you but you say you

87

	haven't in fact been down here for several weeks.
GUY:	That's true.
HESTON:	You've also told me that the reason you came here last night was because your wife telephoned you and asked you to meet her here.
GUY:	(*Tensely*) Yes.
HESTON:	(*Quite simply, facing GUY:*) But your wife's dead, sir. She was murdered ...
GUY:	Yes, I know that.
HESTON:	Well, if she's dead ...
GUY:	(*Agitated*) Look, I've told you, I'll explain all this to Inspector Carter – no one else!

HESTON rises.

HESTON:	Very good, sir.
GUY:	I'm sorry, Sergeant, I know you think I'm being evasive.
HESTON:	I think you could be a little more helpful, sir – let's put it that way.
GUY:	(*Shaking his head*) Believe me, there's no point in telling you the full story, Sergeant. You wouldn't believe it anyway.
HESTON:	Will Inspector Carter believe it?
GUY:	I don't know whether he'll believe it or not, but at least he'll understand what I'm talking about.
HESTON:	(*Frostily*) I hope so, sir.

The DOCTOR appears in the doorway: he is holding the pair of gloves.

DOCTOR:	(*To HESTON*) I'm through ...
HESTON:	Right.

The DOCTOR holds up the gloves.

DOCTOR:	I'd like to take these down to the lab, if I may?
HESTON:	Yes, please do that, sir.

HESTON joins the DOCTOR, and they move out into the hall. GUY crosses to a table and helps himself to a cigarette: he looks tired and overwrought.

HESTON returns as GUY lights his cigarette. GUY looks at him.

GUY: Was she strangled?

HESTON nods.

GUY: What about the gloves? Do you think they were worn by …?

HESTON: (*Quietly: watching GUY*) We're not sure: not yet, sir.

GUY: They were always kept in the hall. I – I used to use them in the garden – just for pottering about …

HESTON: (*Still watching GUY*) I understand, sir.

GUY: I don't think anyone else knew they were there. (*Thoughtfully*) Except Melissa, of course …

CUT TO: The Living Room of GUY's Flat. Morning.

It is eleven o'clock in the morning and GUY – tired, unshaven, and still wearing the same suit – is being interviewed by INSPECTOR CARTER.

CARTER: … Mr Foster, do you really expect me to believe that you thought it was your wife on the phone?

GUY: Yes – Yes, I do.

CARTER tries to control his irritation.

CARTER: But your wife's dead, sir.

GUY: Inspector, I know it must be very difficult for you to understand, but – I was depressed, I'd been drinking, and I was in a very emotional state. Suddenly, out of the blue, I heard Melissa's voice.

CARTER: But it couldn't have been her voice, sir.

GUY: (*Tensely*) Well, it sounded like it – it sounded
           exactly like it!

CARTER looks at GUY for a moment and then moves down to
where he is sitting.

CARTER: Mr Foster, I'm going to be frank with you, sir. I've
           had a report through from Elvingdale. It's been
           established that you went down there and made
           specific inquiries about the dead girl, Mary
           Antrobus. You spoke to her brother in a local
           hairdressers and you also questioned a man called
           Stockton, a car park attendant.

GUY: No, that's not true!

CARTER: You deny that you spoke to …

GUY: No, no, I don't deny anything! I did go down to
           Elvingdale and I did question … Look, Inspector,
           please let me tell you this from the beginning.
           (*After a momentary hesitation*) Don Page came to
           see me. He brought a deedbox which Melissa, my
           wife, had left in his care some little time ago.
           There were several things in the box including a
           letter addressed to me.

CARTER: From your wife?

GUY: Yes.

CARTER: Go on, sir.

GUY: The letter stated that my wife had been friendly
           with someone called Peter Antrobus and that we
           had in fact quarrelled about this man …

CARTER: Then Dr Swanley was right, sir? You did think
           your wife was having an affair with someone?

GUY: No, no, I'm only telling you what was in the letter.
           (*He shakes his head*) I'd never heard of Peter
           Antrobus until I read Melissa's letter.

CARTER: Go on, sir.

GUY takes a slip of paper out of his pocket.

GUY: Later, someone broke into my flat – well "broke" is hardly the right word, they must have had a key – and left this message on my typewriter.

GUY hands CARTER the slip of paper.

GUY: I went down to Elvingdale fully expecting to see the man that Melissa had been friendly with. Peter Antrobus turned out to be a schoolboy, a boy of about twelve. Naturally, I was bewildered, and I made inquiries about the whole family. That's how I met Mary Antrobus.

CARTER: I see.

CARTER looks at the message.

CARTER: You say someone entered your flat and left this on the typewriter?

GUY: Yes.

CARTER: You've no idea who it was?

GUY: (*After a moment*) No, except that I'm pretty sure it was a woman. I found a lace handkerchief by the window. I think she must have been hiding behind the curtain.

CARTER: Have you the handkerchief?

GUY crosses and takes the handkerchief out of a drawer in the desk. The INSPECTOR takes it and examines it.

GUY: When I saw the initial on it I thought for a moment … (*He hesitates*)

CARTER: (*Quietly; he looks up*) Yes, I can imagine what you thought, sir.

CARTER looks at the handkerchief again.

CARTER: Now you're quite sure you've told us the truth about Elvingdale?

GUY: Yes.

CARTER: You didn't go down there to see Mary Antrobus?

GUY shakes his head.

CARTER: To arrange a meeting with her later, at the cottage?

GUY: No, I didn't. I didn't even know the girl existed.

CARTER: Did you see anyone else in Elvingdale, apart from Mary Antrobus and her brother?

GUY: Yes, I bumped into Joyce Dean, Dr Swanley's secretary. She was coming out of a shop; I was on my way to the car park.

CARTER: (*Obviously interested*) What was she doing down there, do you know?

GUY: She told me she used to live in Elvingdale, apparently her mother still does.

CARTER: Was she alone?

GUY: No, Dr Swanley's chauffeur was with her. It rather looked as if she'd borrowed the car for the day.

CARTER: I see.

CARTER looks thoughtfully, then suddenly puts the handkerchief in his pocket.

CARTER: Now sir, if you don't mind, I'd like to see that letter – the one that was in the deedbox.

GUY returns to the desk and opening the bottom drawer takes out the deedbox. He takes keys from his pocket, unlocks the box, and looks for the letter.

CARTER: (*Watching GUY*) Can't you find it, sir?

GUY: (*Puzzled*) No, it doesn't appear to be here. That's very funny, I'm sure I put it back in the box …

GUY opens a drawer and takes out several manuscripts.

GUY: Ah, here we are …

GUY produces a letter and hands it to CARTER.
The INSPECTOR reads it.
There is a long pause.

CARTER looks at GUY, then returns the letter to GUY without speaking.

GUY: (*Puzzled*) What is it?

CARTER indicates the letter.

CUT TO the letter in GUY's hand. We read:

"Dear Guy,

I'm sorry I had to hurt you like this. It was always my hope that you wouldn't find out what happened that night, but – please don't think too badly of me ...

Melissa ..."

GUY stares at the INSPECTOR obviously bewildered.

CARTER: That letter doesn't mention Peter Antrobus. It doesn't mention anyone by name.

GUY: But – but it did. I can assure you of it ...

GUY turns the letter over in his hand.

CARTER: Is that the same letter, sir?

GUY: Why, yes, it looks exactly the same ... But it can't be!

CARTER: (*Quietly, obviously not believing GUY*) There's hardly likely to be two, sir.

CARTER moves to GUY and takes the letter from him.

CARTER: Did Mr Page see the letter?

GUY: Yes – yes, he did.

CARTER nods, puts the letter in his wallet, and slowly picks up his hat from the settee.

CARTER: Then I'll have a word with him.

CARTER moves towards the hall.

CARTER: I take it you're not going away, Mr Foster? You'll be in Town for the next day or two?

GUY: Yes, of course.

CARTER nods.

CARTER: Just in case I want to get in touch, sir. It's all right, I can let myself out.

CARTER goes out into the hall.

After a moment, we hear the front door open and close.

CUT TO: DR SWANLEY's Consulting Room, Wimpole Street. Day.
SWANLEY is sitting at his desk writing a letter. JOYCE DEAN comes into the room carrying a manilla folder and a cup of tea. She puts the cup of tea down on the desk and crosses to the filing cabinet near the window.
SWANLEY: (*Not looking up*) Thank you.
JOYCE opens the cabinet and starts to arrange the files, finally inserting the one she is carrying. SWANLEY is still writing his letter.
SWANLEY: What time is Mrs Stephenson coming?
The telephone rings.
JOYCE: Four-thirty.
SWANLEY: (*Lifting the receiver*) It's all right, I'll take it. It's probably the clinic. (*On the phone*) Hello?

CUT TO: A Corner of CHIEF-INSPECTOR CARTER's Office: Scotland Yard. Day.
CARTER is on the telephone, sitting at his desk.
CARTER: Dr Swanley?
SWANLEY: Speaking ...
CARTER: Good afternoon, sir. I'm sorry to disturb you – this is Inspector Carter.

CUT TO SWANLEY:
SWANLEY: (*Surprised*) Oh, good afternoon, Inspector.
JOYCE turns and looks across at the DOCTOR.

CUT TO CARTER:
CARTER: Doctor, I'm making inquiries about a girl called Mary Antrobus and I think perhaps your secretary might be able to help me.

94

SWANLEY: My secretary.

CARTER: Yes. (*Pleasantly: almost a sudden thought*) Or perhaps you can help me, Doctor?

CUT TO SWANLEY:

SWANLEY: I will if I can, certainly. What is it you want to know?

CARTER: I understand you went down to Elvingdale on Saturday, sir?

SWANLEY: No, I didn't go down there. My secretary did.

CUT TO CARTER:

CARTER: Oh, I see. I'm sorry, Doctor, someone said they'd seen your car and chauffeur in the village, and I naturally thought …

CUT TO SWANLEY:

SWANLEY: That's quite right, they did. My chauffeur drove Miss Dean down there on Saturday morning. Her mother lives in Elvingdale and she hasn't been very well. But why not have a word with my secretary, she's here now?

CARTER: Oh, thank you, sir.

SWANLEY offers JOYCE the receiver.

SWANLEY: (*To JOYCE*) It's Inspector Carter, he'd like to talk to you.

JOYCE looks at SWANLEY, hesitates a fraction of a second, then takes the phone.

JOYCE: (*On the phone*) Miss Dean speaking …

CUT TO CARTER:

CARTER: (*Very friendly*) Good afternoon, Miss Dean, I'm sorry to disturb you but I'm hoping you might be able to help me. Did you, by any

95

chance, bump into a girl called Mary
Antrobus while you were in Elvingdale?

CUT TO JOYCE:

JOYCE: (*Puzzled*) No, I'm afraid I didn't.

CARTER: But you know the young lady I'm referring
            to?

JOYCE: Yes, I do. Her father has a garage just outside
            the village.

CUT TO CARTER:

CARTER: That's quite right. I'm trying to gather as
            much information as I can about Miss
            Antrobus, and since I understand she was by
            way of being a friend of yours …

CUT to JOYCE:

JOYCE: (*Curtly*) She's not a friend of mine. We
            hardly know each other. We met once, about
            a year ago, that's all.

CUT TO CARTER:

CARTER: (*Apologetically*) Oh, I see! Well, in that case,
            I beg your pardon, Miss Dean. I appear to
            have been misinformed. So sorry to have
            troubled you …

CUT TO JOYCE:

JOYCE: (*Stopping CARTER*) But why are you
            interested in Mary Antrobus? Has something
            happened to her?

CUT TO CARTER:

CARTER: I'm afraid it has. She was found dead, early this morning.

JOYCE: Where?

CARTER: In a cottage near Lenton-on-Sea. She was strangled. Curiously enough the cottage belongs to a patient of Dr Swanley's. Mr Foster.

CUT TO JOYCE:

JOYCE: Mr Foster ...?

CUT TO CARTER:

CARTER: Yes ... (*Pleasantly*) Well, again – my apologies, Miss Dean. Sorry to have bothered you. Goodbye. (*He replaces his receiver*)

CUT TO JOYCE who replaces the receiver. She looks across at DR SWANLEY. SWANLEY stares back at her, imperturbable, quietly stirring his cup of tea.

CUT TO: The Living Room of GUY's Flat. Evening.
GUY is sitting at his desk, working on his novel. He is stirring a cup of coffee. He sips the coffee as he corrects the manuscript and makes an occasional note on a scribbling pad. The door bell rings. GUY looks up, puts down his pen, and goes out into the hall.

CUT TO: The Front Door of GUY's Flat. Evening.
DON PAGE is standing at the door, his finger on the bell push. He wears a dark coat over a dinner jacket and looks distinctly irritated. The door opens.

GUY: (*Surprised*) Why, hello, Don!

DON: Guy, I'd like to see you. May I come in?

GUY: Yes, of course.

DON: (*Suddenly hesitating*) Are you alone?

GUY: (*Puzzled by DON's manner*) Yes, I'm alone.

DON nods and enters the flat.

CUT TO: The Living Room of GUY's Flat. Evening.

DON enters followed by GUY.

GUY: Let me take your coat.

DON: No, I can only stay a few minutes, I'm going out to dinner. Guy, why the hell did you tell the Inspector about the deedbox?

GUY: About the deedbox?

DON: Yes. You told the Inspector that Melissa gave me the box and asked me to keep it for her.

GUY: But she did.

DON: Yes, old boy, but you didn't have to tell Carter that! Now the damn fool's labouring under the delusion that your wife and I were having ... well, that we were extremely friendly – that I knew everything about her in fact.

GUY: (*Quietly*) I don't think either of us knew everything about Melissa.

DON: No, well you try telling the Inspector that!

GUY: I'm afraid I had to tell Carter about the box, Don.

DON: But you didn't have to tell him that I brought it here! You could have simply said it was Melissa's.

GUY: Don, I don't think you understand. A girl called Mary Antrobus ...

DON: (*Interrupting GUY*) I know all about Mary Antrobus; Carter came to see me this afternoon. He questioned me about that letter – the one you read out to me.

GUY: (*Anxiously*) You told him you saw the letter, of course – that it was in the box?

98

DON:	Yes, of course I did. But I didn't actually see what was in the letter, old boy.
GUY:	You didn't?
DON:	No, of course I didn't. You remember – you read it out to me.
GUY:	Yes, but you know what was in it! You know perfectly well that it mentioned someone called Peter Antrobus and that …
DON:	(*Uncomfortably*) Look, Guy, the Inspector questioned me in great detail about that letter. I had to tell him the truth.
GUY:	(*Angrily*) Of course you had to tell him the truth, the same as I had to tell him the truth about the deed box.
DON:	Yes, well the truth is, I don't really know whether the letter mentioned anyone called Antrobus or not …
GUY:	(*Facing DON*) What did you tell the Inspector?
DON:	I told him that I saw the letter, it was in the deedbox. He asked me whether I'd actually read the letter, myself. I said I hadn't.
GUY:	Don, I don't think you understand how important this is to me! I went down to Elvingdale because the letter mentioned someone called Peter Antrobus and I was given to understand …
DON:	Yes, I appreciate that, old boy!
GUY:	Well don't you realise, if the Inspector thinks I'm lying about the letter, then he'll naturally assume that I went to Elvingdale for a completely different reason.
DON:	What reason?
GUY:	To see Mary Antrobus.
DON:	Oh … (*Thoughtfully*) Oh, I see.

GUY: Good God, man, put yourself in my shoes! The girl's found dead in my cottage, approximately twenty miles from Elvingdale where she lives. The police know I went to Elvingdale, they know I interviewed the girl. Naturally, they want to know why.

DON: (*Quietly*) I see your point.

GUY: Let's face it, even if I substantiated my story, it still takes a bit of swallowing. I go down to Elvingdale to take a look at a man called Peter Antrobus who was supposed to have been having an affair with my wife. Peter Antrobus then turns out to be the dead girl's brother – a boy of twelve.

DON nods, he looks serious, obviously convinced.

DON: Yes, I can see you're in a spot, old boy.

GUY: I'm in one hell of a spot! Especially now, in view of what you've said about the letter. That didn't exactly help me – old boy.

DON: Yes, but Guy, what else could I have told Carter?

GUY looks at DON and, turning, moves towards the desk.

DON: Guy, what was in the other letter – the one you showed the Inspector?

GUY: It was more or less the same as the first, except that it didn't mention anyone called Antrobus.

DON: And where was it – where did you find it?

GUY: It was in this drawer where I put the first one. (*Thoughtfully*) Although curiously enough, I thought I'd put it back into the deedbox.

DON: Was it in the same handwriting – Melissa's?

GUY: Yes, I'm sure it was.

DON: You haven't got it?

GUY: No, the Inspector took it away with him.

DON nods at GUY then glances at his watch.

DON: Guy, I must make a move. I'm sorry I blew my top off just now, but – well, I'm afraid Carter rather rubbed me up the wrong way when he inferred that Melissa and I were more than just good friends. We weren't, you know. I hope you realise that.

The telephone rings.

DON: (*Indicating the phone*) Take it, old boy. Don't worry about me. I'm off anyway.

DON turns and goes out into the hall. GUY hesitates, not sure whether to show DON out or not, then he decides to answer the phone and picks up the receiver.

CUT TO: A Corner of PAULA HEPBURN's Bedroom. Evening.
PAULA is lying on the bed, telephone in hand. She is wearing a negligee and has obviously just finished polishing her nails.

PAULA: (*Examining her nails*) Guy?

GUY: Who is that?

PAULA: It's Paula …

CUT TO:

GUY: Oh, hello, Paula!

PAULA: Darling, are you doing anything this evening?

GUY: Yes, I'm working, Paula.

CUT TO:

PAULA: Felix is away, he's gone up to Scotland. Why don't you take me out to dinner, Guy?

CUT TO:

GUY: I'd like to, Paula, but I'm afraid I'm not very good company these days, and I've an awful lot of work to do.

PAULA: (*Sympathetically*) Yes, all right, Duckie.

GUY: How long is Felix going to be away?

CUT TO:

PAULA: Oh, he's flying back tomorrow. He's gone up to Edinburgh on business. Business. Ye gods! It'll finish up by costing me a packet, I expect – it always does.

GUY: What is it this time – uranium on the Isle of Skye?

PAULA: No, some fathead's trying to sell him the idea of opening an antique shop.

CUT TO:

GUY: What – Felix?

PAULA: Yes, marvellous, isn't it? I'm the only antique he's got, and he hasn't a clue as to how old I am!

GUY: (*Amused*) Paula, that's the first smile I've had for days.

CUT TO:

PAULA: Yes, I know. (*Seriously*) But watch it, Guy, don't let him talk you into lending him any money.

GUY is faintly surprised by this remark.

GUY: I haven't got any money, Paula – you know that.

PAULA: No, but you will have when Melissa's affairs are straightened out. I'm serious, Duckie – don't lend him a bob! (*She quickly changes the subject*) I'll give you a ring when the old dear gets back.

CUT TO:

GUY: Yes, all right.

PAULA: Bye …

GUY is hesitant, about to say something, but changes his mind.

GUY: Goodbye, Paula.

102

GUY replaces the receiver. He stands for a moment, thoughtfully looking down at the phone, thinking of Paula's remark. After a little while he feels in his pockets for a cigarette then suddenly realises that the front door bell is ringing. He turns and goes out into the hall.

CUT TO: The Hall of GUY's Flat. Evening.
GUY enters the hall, crosses it and opens the front door. Immediately he opens the door a man's fist is thrust forward, hitting him violently on the chest and knocking him backwards, almost into the living room. The owner of the fist – a dark, heavily built man of about fifty-five, quickly hurls himself through the door in pursuit of an astonished GUY.

CUT TO: The Living Room of GUY's Flat. Evening.
GUY staggers back into the living room, pursued by the visitor, who is now holding a revolver.

GUY: What is this? Who the hell are you?

GEORGE: (*Intensely angry*) Don't you know? Can't you guess, Mr Foster?

GUY: (*Tensely*) No, I'm damned if I can! And if you think you can just break in here …

GEORGE: (*Interrupting GUY*) Antrobus. George Antrobus.

GUY stops, stares at the man.

GUY: (*Stunned*) Oh … oh, I see …

GEORGE: (*Moving towards GUY*) Why did you kill my daughter?

GUY: (*Tensely, frightened*) I didn't …

GEORGE: It was your cottage, they found her body in your cottage …

GUY: (*Backing away*) Yes – yes, I know they did …

GEORGE: Twenty four hours before that you were in Elvingdale making inquiries about her. You even asked a car park attendant whether she …

GUY:	Mr Antrobus, please! Please let me explain. (*A moment*) My wife was murdered too – strangled ... exactly like your daughter. I went to Elvingdale because I thought there was someone down there called Antrobus who ... who ...
GEORGE:	(*Quietly, watching GUY*) Go on ...
GUY:	(*Despairingly*) Oh, my God, how can I possibly explain to you? (*Shaking his head*) How in God's name can I even begin?
GEORGE:	If you didn't kill Mary, then who did?
GUY:	I don't know.
GEORGE:	What was she doing at your cottage?
GUY:	(*Turning, tensely*) I don't know, Mr Antrobus – believe me, I don't know.

A pause.

GEORGE:	(*Having apparently reached a decision*) I think you're lying. (*He raises the revolver*) I just don't believe you.
GUY:	All right, then, I'm lying. But tell me this; if I murdered your daughter, why did I send for the police? Why didn't I just jump in the car and get away from Lenton as quickly as possible?
GEORGE:	I don't know why – but I expect you had a reason – a good reason.

GUY looks at GEORGE, then walks slowly until he is standing directly in front of him, the revolver only a few feet away.

| GUY: | You've made your mind up, haven't you? There's nothing I can say ... (*He indicates the revolver*) All right, go ahead. |

GEORGE hesitates, and as he does so the phone rings. GUY looks across at it, so does GEORGE.
There is a pause.

The phone continues to ring.

GUY: Go ahead …

GEORGE looks at GUY, he doesn't move. The phone finally stops ringing.

GEORGE: What did you mean just now about Elvingdale – and someone called Antrobus?

GUY: (*Shaking his head*) You won't believe me …

GEORGE: (*Tensely*) Let me be the judge of that.

GUY: My wife left a letter. It gave the impression she was friendly with someone – someone called Antrobus. That's why I questioned your daughter.

GEORGE: Have you told the police this?

GUY: Yes, I have. They don't believe me either.

GEORGE: Why?

GUY: They don't believe me because … (*A shrug*) I haven't got the letter. (*Suddenly, angrily*) Look, if you're not going to use that damn thing, I'd like a drink. I'd also like to ask you some questions, Mr Antrobus, for a change.

GEORGE: (*Curious*) Questions about what?

GUY: Your daughter.

GEORGE: (*After a moment*) What is it you want to know?

GUY looks at GEORGE, then, turning, walks to the drinks table. He starts to mix himself a Scotch and soda.

GUY: I'm pretty sure that the police think – and I agree with them – that your daughter was murdered by the same person that killed my wife. I also have a horrible suspicion that they share your feelings about me. They think I'm that person. (*Turning, quite simply:*) But I didn't kill my wife because I was in love with her. And I certainly didn't murder your

105

daughter … (*He returns to GEORGE, drink in hand*) Mr Antrobus, I want you to do one of two things. I want you to believe me, or … do what you came here to do and then get to hell out of it!

GEORGE hesitates, then suddenly he lowers the revolver and puts his hand over his eyes. He stands quite still for a moment, then he slowly moves across to the settee and sits down. He looks tense and drawn. GUY crosses to him, offering the drink.

GUY: Drink this …

GEORGE takes the glass and drinks. GUY watches him for a second, then he returns to the table and proceeds to mix another drink.

GUY: Mr Antrobus, could you do something for me? Could you make me a list of your daughter's friends? Not just close, personal friends – but people she knew, people she used to talk about?

GEORGE: I could try, but I'm afraid Mary had so many friends. People I just know nothing about.

GUY: Do you happen to know whether she was friendly with a man called Don Page?

GEORGE: (*Surprised*) The racing driver?

GUY: Yes.

GEORGE: (*Puzzled*) No, I don't think so. I don't believe they ever met. (*Shaking his head*) I'm sure she'd have told me if she'd ever met Don Page. He was quite an idol of hers. Don Page. Jim Clark. Stirling Moss.

GUY moves down to the settee.

GUY: Did she ever mention a Doctor Swanley to you?

GEORGE: No.

GUY: Or his secretary, Joyce Dean?

GEORGE: That name sounds familiar. Didn't she work in Elvingdale for a time?

GUY: Yes, at the local hospital.

GEORGE: (*Nodding*) Mary knew her. (*Thoughtfully*) I don't think they were friends though; but they'd certainly met.

GUY: And what about the name Hepburn – Felix and Paula Hepburn?

GEORGE: No, I've certainly never heard that name … (*He stops, a sudden thought has occurred to him*) Felix?

GUY: (*Watching GEORGE*) Yes …

GEORGE: Mary knew someone called Felix. I'm afraid I don't know his other name … I walked into the office about a week ago. She was on the phone. I heard her say … "All right, Felix, let's make it the twenty-fourth …"

GUY: And you've no idea who she was talking to?

GEORGE: No, I'm sorry, I haven't. (*He rises*) This man you've just mentioned. Felix – Hepburn, did you say?

GUY: Yes.

GEORGE: Who is he? What does he do?

GUY: Well, he calls himself a financial consultant, but it's difficult to say what he does, exactly. He's married to a woman called Paula, quite a wealthy woman. My wife knew them both, very well.

GEORGE: Is he a friend of yours?

GUY looks down at his glass, it is difficult to tell whether he is hesitating or not.

GUY: (*Nodding*) Yes, he's a friend of mine.

CUT TO: The Living Room of GUY's Flat. Morning.

It is eleven o'clock the following morning. GUY is sitting at his desk, typing. He finishes the page and is making corrections with a pencil when he suddenly notices that the bracelet attached to his watch has snapped. He slips off his watch and is examining the bracelet when the phone rings. He puts the watch down on the desk and picks up the receiver.

GUY: Guy Foster speaking ...

CUT TO: An old-fashioned roll top desk in the corner of a room.

The desk is open and we see a mass of papers, note books, pencils, ball pens, etc.

GEORGE is standing by the desk, telephone in one hand, a pipe in the other.

GEORGE: This is George Antrobus ... Mr Foster, you
                remember our conversation last night about
                that friend of yours, Felix Hepburn?

CUT TO:

GUY: Yes?

GEORGE: He <u>was</u> the man on the phone – the man Mary
                was talking to.

GUY: How do you know?

CUT TO:

GEORGE: This morning Peter – my son – found a note
                in Mary's handwriting. I'll read you what it
                says.

GEORGE moves to the front of the desk and puts down his pipe.

GEORGE: She scribbled a date on it – Jan. 24th ...

CUT TO:

GUY: The 24th? That's today?

GEORGE: Yes ... it says: Nine o'clock. Felix H. and M. must be there.

GUY: M? Are you sure it says M?

GEORGE: Yes. I'm positive.

GUY: Does it say anything else?

GEORGE: Well, there's two words underneath the date ... The something or other ... Dial, I think it is ...

GUY: The Dial?

GEORGE: Yes, I think so –

GUY: What is that – a pub?

CUT TO:

GEORGE: If it is I've never heard of it.

GUY: Well – what is it?

GEORGE: I don't know ...

GUY: I suppose it could be a meeting place?

GEORGE: Yes, I suppose it could be. I don't know where it is though. (*Thoughtfully*) There's a monument at Carlston Heath, or rather just outside. I believe they call that The Dial, but I'm not really sure.

GUY: Carlston Heath?

GEORGE: It's about twenty-five miles from here. Between Elvingdale and Sutton Lentworth.

GUY: Oh, yes – I think I know it. Mr Antrobus, did your daughter often write notes like this?

GEORGE: Yes, she did, and she left them all over the place. It was a family joke. Mary always said she had a terrible memory. I don't think she had, it was just a habit she got into.

GUY:	Well, I agree with you about Felix Hepburn – she must have known him. The Felix H. is too big a coincidence.
GEORGE:	Would it be a good idea if you phoned him and without saying anything about ...
GUY:	I'm afraid I can't at the moment, he's in Scotland somewhere. (*An afterthought*) At least, he's supposed to be ... (*Suddenly*) Look, leave this with me, Mr Antrobus – for the time being at any rate.
GEORGE:	Yes, all right.
GUY:	What's your phone number, just in case –?
GEORGE:	Elvingdale 84 ...
GUY:	(*Scribbling the number down*) 84 ... Right ... Goodbye – thanks for ringing.

GUY replaces the receiver and quickly rises from the desk. He picks up a packet of cigarettes and takes out his lighter. He looks tense and thoughtful as he lights the cigarette.

CUT TO: The Entrance to a watch repair shop, Baker Street, London. Afternoon.

GUY's Hillman is parked outside of the shop. GUY comes out of the shop and crosses to the car. He is wearing dark grey trousers and a suede jacket. He unlocks the car, jumps in, and drives away.

CUT TO: A Country Road near Carlston Heath, Kent. Night.

GUY's car drives along the road and draws to a standstill near a MAN who is sitting on a gate at the entrance to a field. The MAN is bouncing a rubber ball up and down in front of a frisky puppy. GUY winds down the car window.

GUY:	Am I right for Carlston Heath?
MAN:	A mile and a half, straight on ...

110

GUY: Thank you. I'm looking for a monument. I think it's called The Dial.

MAN: That's right. It's up on the top. You'll see it – you can't miss it …

GUY nods and closes the car window.

CUT TO: The Dial. A War Memorial on Carlston Heath. Kent. Night.

The memorial is on top of the heath; a grey, sombre looking stone with a tiny wall protecting it from trespassers. A path leads up to The Dial from the country lane which runs parallel with the heath. GUY's car is parked in this lane.

GUY is sitting in the car, watching the path along to the memorial. Music is coming from the car radio. He takes a small sports watch out of his pocket and looks at it. It is ten minutes to nine.

CUT TO: As before. It is an hour later.

There are clouds in the sky, the night is darker.

GUY is in his car, watching the war memorial, the radio still playing. Two indistinct figures – a MAN and a WOMAN emerge from the shadows of the memorial and walk down the path towards the country lane. They are walking arm in arm, their heads close together in intimate conversation.

GUY leans forward switching off the radio, intent on watching the approaching couple. When they are about twenty yards or so from the car he switches on the headlights, the MAN and his GIRLFRIEND are taken completely by surprise, quickly shielding their eyes from the sudden glare of the lights. GUY switches off the lights.

CUT TO: As before.

GUY is still sitting in the car; the radio is on. He looks at his watch – it is half past eleven. He hesitates, not quite sure what

111

to do, then he suddenly makes a decision and turns the ignition key.

CUT TO: The Living Room of GUY's Flat. The following morning.
GUY comes out of the bedroom and goes out into the hall. He is wearing pyjamas and a dressing gown and has obviously only just got out of bed.

CUT TO: The Hall of GUY's Flat. Morning.
GUY opens the front door of his flat and picks up a bottle of milk, and the morning newspaper. He is about to close the door when the newspaper headline catches his eye, and he stands by the half open door staring in amazement at the front page of the paper. There is a large photograph of JOYCE DEAN, in nurse's uniform. The words "JOYCE DEAN" appear under the photograph. The headline reads: Nurse brutally attacked in Carlston Heath incident". Guy stares transfixed, at the photograph of JOYCE DEAN.
CARTER's VOICE: May I come in, Mr Foster?
GUY quickly looks up. INSPECTOR CARTER is standing in the doorway.

GUY:	I – I was just reading about … (*He is staggered*) When did this happen?
CARTER:	About half past eleven last night, sir.
GUY:	Is she seriously hurt?
CARTER:	She's very badly shaken, sir. The man tried to strangle her, fortunately he failed, and she was able to get away from him.
GUY:	What was she doing at Carlston Heath?
CARTER:	We don't know. She hasn't really been able to tell us anything yet. And Doctor Swanley can't throw any light on the affair either. He

112

was under the impression she had a theatre date last night.

GUY: Where is she?

CARTER: At the moment she's in the local hospital but I understand the doctor's bringing her back to Town this morning.

GUY nods, looks at the newspaper again. He is quietly stunned, uncertain what to say or do. The INSPECTOR looks at him.

CARTER: (*Quietly*) Do you think we might go into the lounge, sir?

GUY: What? Oh, yes – yes, of course.

GUY moves towards the living room then stops dead, turning and looking at the INSPECTOR.

GUY: I went to Carlston Heath last night. I drove out there. I … I … (*He is lost for words*)

CARTER: Yes, I know you did, sir.

CARTER nods towards the living room.

CUT TO: The Living Room of GUY's Flat. Morning.

GUY enters the living room followed by the INSPECTOR.

CARTER: Tell me about last night, Mr Foster.

GUY is still bewildered holding the newspaper.

GUY: I left Town at about half past seven, perhaps a bit later. I got to Carlston Heath about a quarter to nine. I – I parked my car …

CARTER: I know where you parked your car. You've got a Hillman 466 XPJ?

GUY: Yes, that's right.

CARTER: It was parked in the lane facing the monument, about a quarter of a mile from where Miss Dean was attacked.

GUY: I … didn't know that. (*Shaking his head*) I – I
                don't know anything about this business,
                Inspector.

CARTER: Why did you go out to Carlston Heath, Mr
                Foster?

GUY is not quite sure where to begin.

GUY: George Antrobus came to see me. The poor
                devil was angry – intensely angry. He thought
                I'd killed his daughter …

CARTER: Go on, sir.

GUY is obviously worried, not at all sure how to continue.

GUY: Mary Antrobus left a note, apparently she had
                a bad memory and she used to scribble things
                down so that she didn't … forget… them …

CARTER: (*Quietly*) Go on, sir.

*GUY hesitates, then suddenly puts the newspaper down and
faces CARTER.*

GUY: Look, Inspector, you're not going to believe
                me! You're not going to believe me unless …

CARTER: Unless what, sir?

GUY: Unless you come out to Elvingdale with me
                and see George Antrobus.

CARTER: (*Curious*) And why should I do that?

GUY: He's got a note that Mary, his daughter, left.
                If you talk with Antrobus and read that note,
                well – at least you'll know why I went out to
                Carlston Heath last night.

CARTER looks at GUY.

There is a pause.

CARTER: All right, Mr Foster. Let's go out to
                Elvingdale.

CUT TO: GEORGE ANTROBUS's Garage. Elvingdale. Day.

The Hillman drives up to the petrol pump and GUY gets out of the driving seat followed by the INSPECTOR. A tall fair-haired MAN, whom we have never seen before, is standing near a Rover which is parked outside the showrooms. He is talking to a middle-aged WOMAN, the owner of the car. The MAN looks up and sees the INSPECTOR. CARTER gives a casual wave and the MAN nods and calls across to him.

MAN: I'll be with you in a second.

GUY turns towards the INSPECTOR.

GUY: Who's that?

CARTER: (*Puzzled*) Who is it?

GUY: Yes.

CARTER looks at GUY.

CARTER: Why, it's George Antrobus, of course.

GUY: George Antrobus?

GUY stares at the INSPECTOR in astonishment, then quickly looks across at the fair-haired MAN.

END OF EPISODE FOUR

EPISODE FIVE

OPEN TO: GEORGE ANTROBUS's Garage near Elvingdale. Day.

The INSPECTOR is looking at GUY who is staring across at GEORGE ANTROBUS who is still standing near the Rover, talking to the middle-aged WOMAN.

GUY: You say that's George Antrobus?

CARTER: Yes, of course it's George Antrobus! Isn't he the man you told me about? The man who came to your flat?

GUY is bewildered and shakes his head.

GUY: No ...

CARTER: Well, who the devil was ... What was he like, the man you saw?

GUY: He was about the same age, I suppose. Tall, dark ... My God, Inspector – I never dreamt for a second he wasn't Antrobus!

CARTER looks at GUY and then across at ANTROBUS who is obviously now on the verge of saying "Goodbye" to his customer. The INSPECTOR makes a sudden decision.

CARTER: (*To GUY*) Get in the car, drive fifty yards up the road and wait for me. I'll be with you in ten minutes.

GUY: (*Puzzled*) But who do you want me to ...

CARTER: Do as I ask you, Mr Foster, please!

GUY hesitates, then gets into the car. The INSPECTOR quickly turns and walks towards GEORGE ANTROBUS who is saying "Goodbye" to MRS LONG, the owner of the Rover.

ANTROBUS: ... Everything will be laid on, Mrs Long, you've nothing to worry about. I'll pick up the car myself on Tuesday morning.

MRS LONG: Thank you, Mr Antrobus.

MRS LONG gets into the Rover and drives away.

CARTER: Good morning, Mr Antrobus.

GEORGE ANTROBUS turns towards the INSPECTOR: now that his customer has departed his manner changes. He looks what he is: an extremely worried man.

ANTROBUS: Good morning, Inspector. Is there any news?

CARTER: Well – I expect you've seen this morning's paper, sir?

ANTROBUS: (*Curious*) No, I haven't.

CARTER: Someone tried to murder a girl called Joyce Dean. We think it was the same man – we're pretty sure it was in fact.

ANTROBUS: (*Obviously surprised*) When was this?

CARTER: Last night on Carlston Heath. He tried to strangle her, fortunately she put up a fight. Incidentally, Miss Dean's a local girl. I don't know whether you know her or not?

ANTROBUS: We've never met, but I know who you mean. I used to see her about quite a lot when she worked at the hospital.

CARTER: Yes, that's right. She works for a Doctor Swanley at the moment.

ANTROBUS: Rather an ambitious girl, they used to say.

CARTER: Ambitious? In what way ambitious, sir?

ANTROBUS: Oh – it was just gossip. Jealousy, I suppose. The hospital were rather annoyed when she left here and went to work in London.

CARTER: Oh, I see. (*He hesitates, and then:*) Mr Antrobus, had your daughter a very good memory?

ANTROBUS: Yes, I think so – she certainly hadn't a bad one.

CARTER: She didn't make a habit of jotting things down just in case she forgot them?

ANTROBUS: Not to my knowledge. I certainly never remember her doing that.

CARTER *gives a little nod.*

CARTER: May I use your phone?

ANTROBUS *indicates the office.*

ANTROBUS: Yes, of course, help yourself. It's on the desk.

CARTER *moves towards the office door, then stops.*

CARTER: (*Turning*) Mr Antrobus …

ANTROBUS *is puzzled by CARTER's manner, his hesitancy.*

ANTROBUS: Yes, Inspector?

CARTER: (*Quietly*) Did you know that your daughter took drugs?

ANTROBUS: (*Staggered*) Drugs? Mary? …

CARTER: Yes – she'd been taking heroin for almost a year.

ANTROBUS: I – I don't believe this. I just don't believe it!

CARTER: I'm sorry, sir, but it's true. There's a medical report on my desk, it came through this morning.

CARTER *looks at ANTROBUS, obviously sorry for him; he is about to say something else, then changes his mind and opens the office door. ANTROBUS slowly turns towards a YOUNG MAN in a sports car, who has just driven up.*

CUT TO: The Garage Office. Music.

CARTER *enters the office and crosses to the telephone. He picks up the receiver and dials: as he does so his eyes rest for a moment on the photograph of DON PAGE which still stands on the corner of the desk.*

CUT TO: DETECTIVE SERGEANT GIBBS' Office. Scotland Yard. Day.

GIBBS *is sitting at his desk finishing off a report. The phone rings.*

GIBBS: (*On the phone*) Extension 193 … Sergeant Gibbs.

121

CARTER:	(*On the other end of the phone*) Carter …
GIBBS:	Oh, good morning, sir! I've been trying to get in touch with you.

CUT TO:

CARTER:	I'm out at Elvingdale. What happened? Have you seen Miss Dean?
GIBBS:	Yes, I've just got back, sir. She's very much better, made quite a good recovery in fact.
CARTER:	Did you get a description from her?

CUT TO:

GIBBS:	Yes, I did, sir. She said the man was about five feet ten, clean shaven, dark, and was apparently wearing a suede jacket of some kind.

CUT TO:

CARTER:	She certainly has made a quick recovery. She couldn't remember a damn thing last night. Anything else?
GIBBS:	Yes, she said he wore a bracelet, she felt it while she was struggling with him.
CARTER:	What does she mean – an identity bracelet?
GIBBS:	No, on his wristlet watch, sir – instead of a strap.
CARTER:	Oh, I see. All right, Gibbs. I'll be in touch. Oh – when you interviewed Miss Dean was Doctor Swanley there?

CUT TO:

GIBBS:	Part of the time, sir. He left while I was talking to her.
CARTER:	Right – thank you, Sergeant.

GIBBS puts the phone down.

GIBBS: ... Take that down to Sergeant O'Hara. If he complains he can't read it, tell him he shouldn't be in the C.I.D.

CUT TO: A Country Road near Elvingdale. Day.
GUY's car is parked about fifty yards from the entrance to the ANTROBUS garage. INSPECTOR CARTER is walking towards the car. As he reaches it, GUY leans across and opens the passenger door.

CUT TO: Inside GUY's Car. Day.

CARTER: I've spoken to the Yard. Miss Dean seems very much better, she's made a remarkably quick recovery, in fact.

GUY: Oh, good. I'm glad to hear that.

CARTER: Yes, I thought you would be, Mr Foster. (*Turning towards GUY*) Tell me: what were you wearing last night, sir, when you went out to Carlston Heath?

GUY: What was I wearing? Grey flannel trousers and ... a jacket.

CARTER: An ordinary sports jacket, sir?

GUY: Yes – well, no – actually it's a suede jacket.

CARTER gives a noncommittal nod and glances at his wristlet watch.

CARTER: What time do you make it? I think my watch has stopped.

GUY takes out his pocket watch and looks at it.

CARTER: (*Pleasantly*) I thought you had a wristlet watch, sir, rather a nice one with a bracelet.

GUY: Yes, I have, but unfortunately the bracelet broke yesterday ... (*He stops and looks at the*

123

	INSPECTOR) What is this? Why are you interested in my watch?
CARTER:	(*Briskly*) When did the bracelet break, sir?
GUY:	Yesterday afternoon.
CARTER:	Before you went out to Carlston Heath?
GUY:	Yes.
CARTER:	So you didn't wear the watch last night, sir?
GUY:	No: I couldn't have done.
CARTER:	Why not?
GUY:	(*Faintly irritated*) Well, for two reasons. One, because it was broken, and two because I hadn't got it. I took it to a jewellers in the afternoon to have it repaired.

CARTER looks at GUY.

| CARTER: | (*Suddenly*) Thank you, Mr Foster. Now I'd like to hear a little more about that visitor of yours. The man who called himself George Antrobus. (*Pleasantly, he points through the windscreen*) There's a very nice pub down the road. Suppose you tell me all about it over a glass of beer. |

GUY looks at the INSPECTOR for a moment, obviously puzzled by his manner, then he leans forward and starts the car.

CUT TO: The Saloon Bar of The Brown Owl – a country inn near Elvingdale. Day.

GUY and the INSPECTOR are sitting at a corner table drinking beer: there is a plate of sandwiches in front of them.

CARTER:	… Was the revolver loaded?
GUY:	I don't know whether it was loaded or not. I certainly thought it was at the time.
CARTER:	And you'd definitely recognise the man again?
GUY:	Yes, of course I would.

CARTER:	What time was it when he phoned you?
GUY:	Oh, just after breakfast. He said that Peter, his son, had found the note and that it tied up with the phone call his daughter had made. The one he'd mentioned the day before. My God, he was so convincing, Inspector! I never for a moment suspected he wasn't George Antrobus.
CARTER:	Tell me again, sir. What did he say was in the note?
GUY:	(*Reflecting*) Nine o'clock ... Felix H. and M ...
CARTER:	You thought the Felix referred to Felix Hepburn?
GUY:	Yes.
CARTER:	And the M?

GUY doesn't answer.

CARTER:	You thought the M referred to your wife?
GUY:	(*Hesitantly*) Well – (*He nods*) Yes, I did.
CARTER:	And that's precisely what you were intended to think, sir. (*Leaning forward*) Mr Foster, your wife is dead. Don't let there be any doubt in your mind about that. The body was identified, not only by you, but by several other people as well.
GUY:	(*Tensely*) Yes, I know. I keep telling myself that. But things have been happening – such curious things ...
CARTER:	Such as what, sir?
GUY:	Well, there was the music ... the handkerchief with the initial on it ... then the voice, Melissa's voice, on the phone ...
CARTER:	It couldn't have been your wife's voice.

GUY: Yes, I know now it couldn't have been, but –
                it sounded like Melissa, it sounded exactly
                like her ...

There is a long pause.

CARTER sips his beer and looks at GUY.

CARTER: You've had a pretty rough time just lately,
                haven't you, Mr Foster?

GUY: My God, you can say that again.

There is another pause.

GUY is about to say something then changes his mind.

CARTER: (*Smiling*) Go on, Mr Foster – say it.

GUY: Can I ask you a very frank question?

CARTER: Yes, but you might not get a very frank
                answer.

GUY: (*Looking at CARTER*) Do you think I killed
                my wife?

*CARTER stares back at GUY, then looks at his glass. He
seems to be examining it.*

CARTER: (*Quietly*) No, I don't.

GUY: Why don't you think so?

CARTER: (*Looking up*) Because of something you once
                said to me.

GUY: (*Surprised*) Something I said?

CARTER: Yes. You said your wife used to buy a lot of
                hats, but she hardly ever wore one.

GUY: (*Perplexed*) And that convinced you that I
                didn't kill Melissa?

CARTER: (*With a faint smile*) Yes, sir – that convinced
                me.

CUT TO: The Waiting Room in DOCTOR SWANLEY's
House in Wimpole Street.
This is a waiting room for DR SWANLEY's patients;
furnished with heavy Victorian furniture and with the

conventional "Tally-ho" prints on the walls it offers a complete contrast to the doctor's consulting room.

CARTER is sitting on a chair, legs crossed, trying to ease his right shoe. He is obviously still having trouble with it. There is a sports hat on the arm of the chair opposite him. The door opens and an ELDERLY WOMAN in a nurse's uniform enters.

RECEPTIONIST: Doctor Swanley won't keep you long now, Inspector.

CARTER: Thank you.

As the RECEPTIONIST turns to go out DON PAGE comes in. He is smiling and looks rather pleased with life; the smile fades somewhat when he sees the INSPECTOR.

CARTER: (*Uncrossing his legs; rising*) Good afternoon, Mr Page. This is a surprise, sir.

DON picks up the hat.

DON: I left my hat in here.

CARTER: (*Pleasantly*) Just been having a check-up with Dr Swanley, sir?

DON: Yes, I have, as a matter of fact.

CARTER: I'm glad I bumped into you. I was going to give you a ring. I believe you told Mr Foster that his wife won a great deal of money gambling?

DON: Yes, she did. That's how she bought her jewellery.

CARTER: Did you go gambling with Mrs Foster, sir?

DON: No, that sort of thing doesn't appeal to me. I'm not a gambler.

CARTER: Then how do you know that she was, sir? How do you know that she won all this money gambling?

DON: Because she told me! Besides, if she didn't win it, old boy, where the devil did it come

127

	from? Why, she used to tell me the most amazing stories. She even turned up at my flat one night with seventeen hundred quid – cash.
CARTER:	Seventeen hundred?
DON:	Yes – and do you know how she got it? A friend took her to the races and just as she was … (*He stops; looks at CARTER*) But wait a minute! What is this, Inspector? You know perfectly well that Melissa gambled! She must have done, otherwise …
CARTER:	Mr Page, since I last saw you we've been making extensive inquiries in the West End about Mrs Foster.
DON:	Well?
CARTER:	If, as you suggest, she won large sums of money gambling, how is it that she didn't frequent the usual haunts?
DON:	But she did!
CARTER:	Such as?
DON:	Well – Carrington's Club for instance.
CARTER:	Did Mrs Foster tell you she'd been to Carrington's?
DON:	Yes, several times. She told me she once won nine hundred pounds there.
CARTER:	(*Shaking his head*) That doesn't tie up with our information. We've checked at Carrington's – they'd never heard of her until she was murdered.

DON looks puzzled, a shade worried.

DON:	I don't understand this?
CARTER:	Neither do I, sir. (*Watching GUY*) You say Mrs Foster came to your flat one night and

	she had seventeen hundred pounds with her, in cash?
DON:	Yes.
CARTER:	How did she carry such a large sum of money, not in her handbag, surely?
DON:	No, curiously enough …
CARTER:	… Or perhaps she had a hatbox with her on that occasion, sir?
DON:	Why, yes! (*Surprised, staring at the INSPECTOR*) As a matter of fact she had.

DOCTOR SWANLEY's voice is suddenly heard in the corridor, talking to the RECEPTIONIST.

SWANLEY:	(*Off*) … Mrs Bellinger has changed her appointment. I'm seeing her tomorrow morning.
RECEPTIONIST:	(*Off*) Yes, very good, Doctor.

DOCTOR SWANLEY appears in the doorway. His manner is calm, self-possessed; but in spite of this he looks tired and distinctly worried.

SWANLEY:	I'm very sorry to have kept you waiting, Inspector, but Thursdays are always pretty hectic, I'm afraid.
CARTER:	It's very good of you to see me, without an appointment. (*Pleasantly; dismissing DON*) Goodbye, Mr Page.
DON:	(*Hesitating, then:*) Goodbye, Inspector. Good afternoon, Doctor.
SWANLEY:	Good afternoon. (*To CARTER, as DON goes out*) Would you like to come to my room, or shall we talk here?
CARTER:	We can talk here, sir, if that's all right with you?
SWANLEY:	Yes, of course.

SWANLEY glances at his watch.

CARTER: I shan't keep you long, sir.

SWANLEY: I'm sorry. I didn't mean to be rude, Inspector. (*He indicates a chair*) Please – do sit down.

CARTER returns to his seat, the DOCTOR sits on the arm of the chair opposite him.

SWANLEY: I think I can guess what you want to see me about.

CARTER: I'm a little worried about Miss Dean.

SWANLEY nods.

CARTER: She's given us a very useful description of the man who attacked her, but unfortunately her explanation as to why she went out to Carlston Heath seems a little vague. She's supposed to have received a telegram from an ex-boyfriend, asking her to meet him. Unfortunately, she can't produce the telegram, and, as it turns out, the boyfriend's in Sweden.

SWANLEY: (*Surprised*) In Sweden?

CARTER: Yes, sir. You've no idea why she went out to Carlston Heath, Doctor?

SWANLEY: No, I'm sorry, Inspector, I haven't.

CARTER: What time did she leave here yesterday?

SWANLEY: The usual time – about half-past five.

CARTER: Where did you first meet Miss Dean, Doctor?

SWANLEY: (*After a momentary hesitation*) I met her in Elvingdale about eighteen months ago. I paid a visit to the local hospital, and she introduced herself. She said she wanted to work in Town. Four months later when my secretary left to get married, I remembered Joyce and offered her the job.

CARTER: Quite a lucky break for her?

SWANLEY:	Yes, I suppose it was. But it was a lucky break for me too. She's a pleasant girl and very efficient. I shall be sorry to lose her.
CARTER:	(*Surprised*) Is she leaving you then, Doctor?
SWANLEY:	Why, yes. Didn't you know? She's going to Canada – she leaves me at the end of the week.
CARTER:	(*Quietly; shaking his head*) I didn't know that, sir.
SWANLEY:	Oh, yes. She gave me her notice about a month ago. (*A shrug*) It was a disappointment of course, but there was nothing I could do about it. She's a nice girl, Joyce – but very ambitious. Very.
CARTER:	(*His thoughts apparently elsewhere*) Yes, so I understand, sir.

There is a knock on the door and the RECEPTIONIST appears.

RECEPTIONIST:	I'm sorry, Doctor – but your patient has arrived.

SWANLEY rises.

SWANLEY:	Thank you. (*Holding out his hand*) I'm afraid you'll have to excuse me, Inspector.
CARTER:	Yes, of course.
SWANLEY:	You've got my private number just in case …
CARTER:	(*Shaking hands*) I have indeed, sir.

CUT TO: The Hall of GUY's Flat. Morning.

GUY opens the front door and as he does so PAULA HEPBURN almost falls into his arms. She looks exhausted and frightened; her hair is untidy, her dress torn, a stocking laddered. She holds GUY by the arm, visibly shaking, trying desperately hard to control the tears.

GUY: Paula – what's happened?

PAULA: I – I was knocked down by a car. I came out of a shop and … (*Weakly*) Oh, Guy!

GUY: It's all right, Paula … Don't worry, my dear – come and lie down and let me get you a drink.

PAULA: Wait a minute – please, Guy!

PAULA stands, leaning against the door, trying to regain her composure.

GUY: (*Concerned*) Paula – are you all right?

PAULA: (*Softly*) Yes.

There is a long pause.

GUY: (*Gently*) Do you feel any better?

PAULA gives a little nod, she is obviously recovering.

GUY: When you've had a drink I'll get hold of a doctor, there's a very good one just …

PAULA: No, no, don't worry – I'll be better in a minute!

GUY: Are you sure?

PAULA: (*Forcing a smile*) Yes, Duckie, don't worry …

CUT TO: The Living Room of GUY's Flat. Morning.

GUY enters with PAULA. He helps her across to the settee then crosses down to the drinks table and quickly mixes a brandy and soda.

GUY: (*Returning to settee*) Here, drink this, Paula …

GUY gives PAULA the glass.

PAULA: I don't like brandy, Guy, it always makes me dizzy.

GUY: Yes, I know, but this won't, I've put some soda with it … Now come on, drink up …

PAULA looks at the glass, then drinks.

A pause.

GUY: Well?

132

PAULA: (*Nodding her head*) I feel better; I think it was more shock than anything else ...

GUY: What happened, exactly?

PAULA: I don't know what happened. I was shopping in Oliver Street; you know, that quiet little street just round the corner.

GUY: Yes, I know it.

PAULA: I came out of a shop and was walking towards my car when – a van came out of a side turning. Fortunately, I saw it just in time, otherwise ... (*Shaking her head*) I don't think the van actually hit me, it was just that ... I was so frightened I ran into a cyclist.

GUY: Oh, I see. Did the van stop?

PAULA: No.

GUY: Why – didn't the driver see you?

PAULA: Oh, yes, he saw me – he must have done.

GUY: (*Looking at PAULA*) Then why didn't he stop, I wonder?

PAULA: I don't know.

GUY: Did you get his number?

PAULA: No, I'm afraid I didn't. It all happened so quickly. I – I never even thought about it.

GUY: Well, I'm glad you had the common sense to come round here, Paula.

PAULA: I was on the way home and was feeling pretty awful then I suddenly realised you were just round the corner and ... Guy, do you think I could use the bathroom?

GUY: Good Lord, why yes, of course! How stupid of me!

PAULA: (*Rising from the settee*) It's all right, Duckie, I know where it is.

GUY: I suppose Felix is still in Scotland?

The door bell rings.

PAULA: He's due back this morning. The big deal's off, by the way. He's decided the antique business is a little too old-fashioned for him.

GUY smiles, then turns towards the hall.

PAULA: Are you expecting someone?

GUY: Yes, the Inspector phoned about an hour ago and said he wanted to see me.

PAULA: Oh, Lord! Don't say anything about this business, please, Guy. You know what he's like; he'd keep me here all morning answering questions.

GUY: All right, Paula.

GUY goes out into the hall.

PAULA rises and crosses to the drinks table: she puts her glass down, glances towards the hall, then goes into the bedroom.

We hear the sound of voices and then GUY returns with the INSPECTOR. CARTER carries a briefcase.

CARTER: I won't keep you long, Mr Foster, but I've got some photographs I want you to look at.

GUY: Photographs?

CARTER: Yes. (*He opens his briefcase and takes out some photographs*) We're particularly anxious to identify the gentleman who passed himself off as Mr Antrobus, and these photographs are … (*He stops; looks towards the bedroom*)

GUY: Mrs Hepburn's here – she's in the bedroom.

CARTER: Oh – indeed, sir?

CARTER turns towards the bedroom.

GUY: She was passing and … didn't feel very well.

CARTER: I'm sorry to hear that. It's not serious, I hope?

GUY: No, no, it's not serious.

134

GUY gives the INSPECTOR a little nod, obviously signifying "I'll tell you about it later". CARTER hands GUY a photograph.

CARTER: Just say yes or no, sir.

GUY: *(Looking at the photograph)* No.

GUY returns the photograph to CARTER who hands him another one. GUY looks at the photograph.

GUY: No.

GUY returns the photograph and CARTER, after a momentary hesitation, hands him a third. GUY looks at the photograph, then at CARTER, finally looking at the photograph again. We see the photo is a head and shoulder photograph of GEORGE in prison uniform.

GUY: Yes, definitely.

CARTER smiles and takes the photograph, putting it down with the others on the briefcase. PAULA comes out of the bedroom.

CARTER: *(Turning; pleasantly)* Hello, Mrs Hepburn. I'm sorry to hear you haven't been very well.

PAULA: I was involved in a car accident, nothing very serious – it was rather nasty at the time.

CARTER: Yes, of course. *(Curious)* Was this in London?

PAULA: *(Dismissing the matter)* Yes, but it was nothing, Inspector. Guy, I think I'd like to go home, Duckie, if you don't mind.

GUY: Yes, of course, Paula. Would you like me to drive you home, it won't take me long?

PAULA: No, no, there's no need, really, Guy. I've completely recovered.

GUY takes hold of PAULA's arm.

GUY: I'll take you down. *(To CARTER)* I shan't be a minute, Inspector.

PAULA gives the INSPECTOR a little smile and goes out into the hall with GUY.

CUT TO: Outside GUY FOSTER's Flat. Morning.
PAULA's car, a Karmann Ghia Volkswagen, is parked by the kerb outside GUY's flat. PAULA and GUY come out of the entrance and cross to the car.

GUY: Now are you sure you feel well enough to drive, Paula?

PAULA: Yes, don't worry, dear. I feel very much better. (*Kissing GUY*) You've been very sweet, Guy.

GUY: Nonsense! What are friends for?

PAULA looks at him, as if about to say something, then changes her mind and opens the car door. GUY helps her into the car.

GUY: Now be careful, Paula ...

CUT TO: The Living Room of GUY's Flat. Morning.
CARTER is looking at the photograph of GEORGE when GUY enters from the hall.

GUY: I'm sorry about that, Inspector.

CARTER: What happened to Mrs Hepburn?

GUY: She'd been shopping and was walking back to her car when a van suddenly appeared and nearly knocked her down.

CARTER: Did the van stop?

GUY: No, apparently not. She didn't get the number either.

CARTER: Where was this?

GUY: In Oliver Street. (*Indicating the photograph*) Who is that man?

CARTER:	(*Looking at the photograph*) According to you, sir, he's the man who impersonated George Antrobus.
GUY:	Yes, he is, there's no doubt about that – but who is he?
CARTER:	His name's Pelham – George Pelham, but he uses half a dozen aliases. George Nottingham … Charles Weston … (*A shrug*) You can take your choice.
GUY:	But what does he do?
CARTER:	He's a forger – at least he was until he switched into the confidence racket. We picked him up in fifty-seven for selling a London bus to an unsuspecting Texan. He got three years.
GUY:	But why should he come here and pass himself off as George Antrobus?
CARTER:	Because someone paid him, that's why, Mr Foster. And paid him very handsomely too, that's my guess.
GUY:	You mean someone deliberately paid him to come here and …
CARTER:	They had to find some means of getting you out to Carlston Heath. If Miss Dean was murdered out there and you proved you were somewhere else at the time, they couldn't very well pin the murder on you, now could they, Mr Foster?
GUY:	But Miss Dean wasn't murdered.
CARTER:	No, I know she wasn't.
GUY:	(*Puzzled*) What do you think happened that night?
CARTER:	I'll tell you what I think happened. Someone arranged a meeting with Miss Dean, and they

weren't sure how that meeting was going to turn out. They knew there was a chance that they might have to use force, that they might in fact have to kill her. They had you on tap as a number one suspect.

GUY: But what about Miss Dean – what does she say about all this?

CARTER: She's given us a description of the man, if that's what you mean. A very good description. It fits you like a glove.

GUY: (*Staggered*) Fits me?

CARTER: Yes, sir. Unfortunately, she said you were wearing your wristlet watch at the time.

GUY: But why in God's name should Joyce Dean wish to incriminate me? I've only met the girl twice!

CARTER: I don't know why, sir.

GUY: (*Angrily*) I've a damn good mind to call round on Miss Dean and ask her what the hell she's playing at!

CARTER: You'll have to be quick, sir, she's leaving for Canada at the end of the week. (*Quietly, picking up the photograph of GEORGE*) Can't imagine why she wants to go to Canada. She has a very nice flat: (*He glances at GUY*) Normandy Court, Kensington. Very pleasant. Thirty-five pounds a week, unfurnished.

CUT TO: The Front Door of a Flat in Normandy Court, Kensington, London. Day.
GUY is standing in the carpeted corridor facing the door: his overcoat over his arm, his hat in his hand. He has pressed the

138

bell push and from inside the flat we hear the sound of chimes.

There is a pause.

GUY presses the button again and almost immediately we hear JOYCE calling from inside the flat.

JOYCE: (*Out of vision*) I'm on the phone, I'll be with you in a minute!

There is a pause.

GUY stands waiting; he glances up and down the corridor, then suddenly turns as the front door is opened by JOYCE DEAN. She is wearing a housecoat: a silk scarf covers her throat.

JOYCE: I'm sorry to have kept ...

JOYCE stops: her expression changes – it is obvious that she was expecting someone else.

GUY: I'd like to have a word with you, Miss Dean.

JOYCE: I'm very sorry, Mr Foster, but I'm expecting someone ...

GUY politely pushes past JOYCE and enters the flat.

CUT TO: The Hall of JOYCE DEAN's Flat. Day.

This is a tiny hall with doors leading to the bedroom and lounge. The lounge door is open, and we can see into a bright, attractively furnished room.

JOYCE: (*Annoyed*) I don't think you heard what I said, Mr Foster!

GUY: I heard ... (*Politely*) Can we talk in here?

GUY walks into the main room. JOYCE hesitates, then follows him.

CUT TO: The Lounge of JOYCE DEAN's Flat. Day.

GUY enters and crosses down to a desk and modern style rocking chair; he drops his hat and overcoat onto the chair. JOYCE comes into the room.

JOYCE: (*Angrily*) I'll give you exactly three minutes …
GUY: We shan't need three minutes, Miss Dean, if you tell the truth.
JOYCE: The point is, Mr Foster, will you recognise the truth when you hear it?
GUY: Try me and see.

A moment.

JOYCE: (*Tensely*) What is it you want to know?
GUY: I want to know why you deliberately gave Inspector Carter the impression that it was me who attacked you on Carlston Heath?
JOYCE: I didn't give him that impression. The Sergeant asked me for a description of the man, and I simply gave it to him.
GUY: You knew perfectly well when you gave him that description that you were throwing suspicion onto me.
JOYCE: That's not true!
GUY: (*Quietly*) Who attacked you that night? Who tried to kill you?
JOYCE: (*Shaking his head*) I don't know.
GUY: Do you think it was me?

JOYCE turns away from GUY.

JOYCE: I've told you, I don't know.

GUY suddenly takes hold of JOYCE's arm and swings her round so that she faces him again.

GUY: I'm asking you whether you think it was me?
JOYCE: (*Angry; releasing herself*) I've told you, I don't know whether it was you or not!

There is a pause.

GUY watches JOYCE.

GUY: You look angry, Miss Dean.
JOYCE: I am angry – intensely angry! How dare you come here and deliberately …

140

GUY: But not frightened – not at all frightened, curiously enough.

JOYCE: What do you mean?

GUY: If you thought – if you really thought I was the man who attacked you that night you wouldn't be stood here talking to me like this. You'd be scared – you'd be so God damned scared you'd be raising the roof!

JOYCE: I've never said that you attacked me. I simply gave the Sergeant ...

GUY: You gave the police a description of me. I want to know why?

JOYCE looks tense; worried. She turns away from GUY.

JOYCE: I'm sorry, I – I just don't know what you're talking about. I told the police the truth and there's nothing else I can say.

The door chimes are heard. JOYCE DEAN's visitor has arrived. JOYCE quickly glances towards the hall.

GUY: (*Shaking his head*) You've never told the police the truth. Right from the beginning you've lied – you lied about my visit to Doctor Swanley, you lied about ...

JOYCE: Look, Mr Foster, I'm not going to discuss your visit to Doctor Swanley. If you've got anything to say about that say it to the Inspector, or Doctor Swanley himself, but please, not to me! Now if you'll excuse me ...

JOYCE goes out into the hall, carefully closing the lounge door behind her. GUY stands for a moment staring at the door, then he turns and is about to pick up his hat and coat when his eye falls on a small book which lies open on the desk. This is JOYCE DEAN's private phone book. He moves across to take a better look at the book: suddenly he stiffens. Obviously surprised by what he has seen. He glances towards

141

the hall then quickly picks up the book. We see the open
phone book in GUY's hand. We see a short list of handwritten
names with telephone numbers attached:
Mayfair Laundry: Grosvenor 2191.
Middlesex Hospital: Museum 8333.
Midland Bank: Monarch 0374.
Nottingham (George): Park 0192.
GUY stares at the name NOTTINGHAM in the book.
JOYCE's voice, quiet and intimate, can be heard in the hall.
A door opens and closes.
GUY suddenly makes a decision and slips the book into his
jacket pocket. He is picking up his hat and overcoat when
JOYCE returns from the hall.

JOYCE: (*Curtly*) I'm sorry but you'll have to excuse me, a
          friend of mine has arrived.

GUY nods and crosses towards the hall.

GUY: (*As he reaches the door*) I hope you like Canada,
          Miss Dean – if you make it.

JOYCE: (*Tensely; annoyed*) What do you mean? Why
          shouldn't I make it?

GUY turns and looks at JOYCE.

GUY: You tell me …

GUY goes out into the hall. JOYCE stares after him.

CUT TO: The Main Entrance of Normandy Court.
Kensington. London. Day.
GUY comes out of the block of flats and looks up and down
the road in search of a taxi; he is carrying his overcoat over
his arm. Suddenly, he sees a taxi in the distance and hails it.
He crosses into the road to join the taxi and as he does so he
becomes aware of a car parked about twenty yards or so from
the entrance to the flats. It is PAULA's Volkswagen. GUY
walks across to the car and looks at it; he is not sure whether

it is PAULA's car or not. The taxi draws level with GUY and after a moment he turns and opens the door.

CUT TO: Inside the Taxi.
GUY is looking at the phone book; turning the pages, carefully scrutinising the names and phone numbers.

CUT TO: The Living Room of GUY's Flat. Afternoon.
INSPECTOR CARTER is examining the phone book. GUY is standing, watching him.

CARTER: (*Looking up*) You know, you really shouldn't have taken it, sir.

GUY: I know I shouldn't have taken it, but what would you have done under the circumstances, Inspector?

CARTER: (*Clearing his throat*) Yes, well – tell me about the visitor – was it a man or a woman?

GUY: (*Hesitantly*) Well – if you must know I think it was Paula Hepburn. But I didn't see her – whoever it was they were shown straight into the bedroom.

CARTER: Then what makes you think it was Mrs Hepburn, sir?

GUY: Her car was outside; I saw it when I left. At least, I think it was her car.

CARTER: You're not sure?

GUY: Well, yes – I'm pretty sure.

CARTER looks at GUY for a moment, then glances down at the book again.

CARTER: You've been through this, of course?

GUY: Yes, there's only two names I recognise, apart from our friend Nottingham or Pelham, or whatever he calls himself.

CARTER: Mary Antrobus and Don Page?

143

GUY:	Yes.
CARTER:	(*Indicating the book*) What about Carol Stewart?
GUY:	Carol Stewart? Is she in there?
CARTER:	(*Reading from the phone book*) Carol … Sloane … 0181. That's Miss Stewart.
GUY:	I didn't realise that. She's the girl Don Page took home, the one that made a nuisance of herself at the party?
CARTER:	That's right.
GUY:	Well, if Carol Stewart's a friend of Joyce Dean's it's my bet she also knows Doctor Swanley.
CARTER:	Yes, that's possible, sir, but I don't quite see where it gets us. (*Thoughtfully*) But it's certainly an interesting coincidence that Miss Dean should be acquainted with Mr Page, Mary Antrobus, and Miss Stewart. (*He looks at the book and crosses to the desk*) Mr Foster, may I use your phone?
GUY:	Yes, certainly.

CARTER picks up the receiver and dials.

CUT TO: DETECTIVE SERGEANT STAFFORD's Office. Day.

The telephone is ringing on the SERGEANT's desk. STAFFORD picks up the receiver.

STAFFORD: Extension 193 … Sergeant Stafford speaking …

CUT TO:

CARTER: Sergeant – Carter. Any news of Pelham?

STAFFORD: No, I'm afraid not, sir. We've checked all his usual haunts. So far, no good.

CARTER:	Well, listen – he's got a number, Park 0192. Check the number, find out where it is. I think you'll find he's using the name Nottingham, George Nottingham – he's used it before.

CUT TO:

STAFFORD:	Right, sir!
CARTER:	And watch it, Stafford! This man's no fool ...
STAFFORD:	Very good, sir. Oh, a Mr Hepburn phoned; he said he wanted to have a word with you. It sounded urgent so I told him you were with Mr Foster.

CUT TO:

CARTER:	What time was this?
STAFFORD:	About half an hour ago.

CARTER is quiet; his thoughts elsewhere.

CARTER:	Thank you, Sergeant.

The INSPECTOR replaces the receiver and moves away from the desk. He looks at GUY, then at the phone book which is now in his hand again.

CARTER:	You say this was on the desk in the lounge?
GUY:	Yes.
CARTER:	Did she see you take it?
GUY:	No.
CARTER:	You're sure?
GUY:	Quite sure.

The door bell is ringing.

CARTER:	(*Nodding towards the hall*) That's probably Mr Hepburn.
GUY:	Felix?
CARTER:	Yes, he's been trying to get in touch with me. He phoned my office about half an hour ago.
GUY:	Oh, I see.

145

CARTER: If it is Mr Hepburn, sir, don't say anything about this book.

GUY looks at the INSPECTOR, then goes out into the hall. CARTER slips the phone book into his pocket, sits on the arm of the settee, and commences to ease his right shoe. Voices are heard in the hall.

FELIX: (*Off; agitated*) ... I tried to get him at the office, but a chap called Stamford, or Stafford, or some damn silly name like that said he was probably with you, old boy ...

GUY: (*Off*) Yes, he is. Come along in, Felix.

GUY enters with FELIX who looks flustered and faintly obstreperous.

CARTER: Good afternoon, Mr Hepburn. I understand you've been trying to get in touch with me?

FELIX: Yes, I have. I'm very worried, Inspector. Devilishly worried, if you must know.

CARTER: What is it you're worried about, sir?

FELIX looks at GUY, then at the INSPECTOR.

FELIX: Someone's trying to kill my wife.

GUY: Trying to kill Paula?

FELIX: Yes, there's been two attempts. One this morning and one ...

CARTER: We know about the accident in Oliver Street, sir, but surely you're not suggesting that ...

FELIX: (*Annoyed*) That was no accident! It was a deliberate cold-blooded attempt to run my wife down – fortunately, thanks to Paula's presence of mind, it failed.

GUY: And the other attempt, Felix?

FELIX: (*Irritated*) What?

GUY: You said there'd been two attempts.

FELIX: That's right, old boy. There has.

CARTER: Well, when was the first one, sir?

146

FELIX: (*A note of sarcasm*) Can't you guess, Inspector?
CARTER looks puzzled; he shakes his head.

FELIX: (*Almost reprimandingly*) You know, you really
           ought to have thought of this – you really ought
           to have thought of it a long time ago, my dear
           fellow.

CARTER: What do you mean, sir?

FELIX: (*To GUY*) You know what I mean, don't you,
           Guy?

GUY: (*Irritated by FELIX*) No, I'm damned if I do!

FELIX: (*To GUY; significantly*) What was Melissa
           wearing the night she was murdered?

GUY: You know perfectly well what she was wearing!
           She'd borrowed Paula's coat because ... (*He
           stops and stares at FELIX*) Paula's coat ...? You
           mean the murderer thought that ... (*Stunned*) My
           God, he murdered the wrong woman!

FELIX: That's right, my old dear. (*He looks across at the
           INSPECTOR*) He murdered the wrong woman!

END OF EPISODE FIVE

EPISODE SIX

OPEN TO: The Living Room of GUY FOSTER's Flat. Afternoon.

The INSPECTOR is looking at GUY, faintly amused by the expression on his face as he stands facing FELIX.

FELIX: … If you stop to think about it it's perfectly obvious, old boy. It was a dark night, Melissa was wearing Paula's coat, the murderer was in a hurry …

CARTER: How do you know he was in a hurry, sir?

FELIX turns to look at CARTER.

FELIX: What?

CARTER: I said: how do you know he was in a hurry?

FELIX: Well, damn it, don't be stupid, old boy – we can take that for granted, surely?

CARTER: I'm sorry, sir, but we can't take anything for granted – least of all the assumption that Mrs Foster was murdered by mistake. (*He moves down to his hat which is on the settee*) Besides, don't you think we thought of that possibility when we discovered she was wearing someone else's coat? (*Smiling*) We're pretty dense, I know, Mr Hepburn – but not quite that sense, sir.

CARTER picks up his hat.

FELIX: All right – then how do you account for what happened this morning?

CARTER: It was probably just an accident. The van driver realised your wife wasn't hurt and didn't bother to stop. (*A shrug*) I'm afraid that sort of thing happens far too often these days. (*To GUY*) Goodbye, Mr Foster, and thank you for the information you gave me.

CARTER crosses to the hall, then stops – a sudden thought has apparently occurred to him.

151

CARTER: (*To FELIX*) Oh, I've been meaning to ask Mr
Page about this – but perhaps you can help me,
sir?

FELIX: I will if I can.

CARTER: I understand that Miss Stewart – Carol Stewart
– made rather a nuisance of herself at the party
and that Mr Page had to take her home.

FELIX: Yes, that's right. She had too much to drink;
she was argumentative. (*To GUY*) And she
would keep doing that corny old act of hers.

CARTER: Yes, that's what Mr Page said. What is her act,
exactly?

GUY: (*To CARTER*) Impersonations – impressions of
well-known people ...

FELIX: What do you mean – well-known people? You
mean people who have been dead and buried
for the last fifty years!

CARTER: (*Laughing*) I see what you mean, sir.

FELIX: She's a little bitch – an absolute little bitch.
There's no doubt about it, is there, Guy?

GUY: If you say so, Felix.

FELIX: I certainly do say so! That woman's ruined
more parties than anyone I know!

CARTER: (*Smiling*) Thank you, Mr Hepburn. Goodbye,
sir.

CARTER goes out into the hall, followed by GUY.

CUT TO: The Living Room of GUY FOSTER's Flat.
Morning.
*GUY comes out of the bedroom wearing a dressing gown and
pyjamas. He yawns, stretches his arms, and goes out into the
hall.*

152

CUT TO: The Hall of GUY FOSTER's Flat. Morning.

GUY enters the hall and opens the front door. INSPECTOR CARTER hands him a bottle of milk and the morning newspaper.

GUY: (*Surprised*) Oh … Oh, hello, Inspector! You should have stayed the night.

CARTER enters the hall.

CARTER: I might have missed some pretty exciting news if I had have done, sir.

CARTER closes the door. He and GUY move towards the living room.

CARTER: Thanks to you we've picked up George Pelham.

CUT TO: The Living Room of GUY FOSTER's Flat. Morning.

GUY enters with the INSPECTOR.

GUY: What happened, Inspector?

CARTER: We checked that number – the one that was in Miss Dean's phone book. It turned out to be a hotel at Notting Hill Gate. We picked up Pelham at half past three this morning.

GUY: Did you ask whether he came here and whether …?

CARTER: (*Nodding*) Pelham's admitted he passed himself off as Antrobus; he's also confessed to writing that letter – the one found in the deedbox.

GUY: But Melissa wrote that letter; she must have done – it was her handwriting!

CARTER: Mr Foster, George Pelham used to forge banknotes – copying your wife's handwriting was child's play.

GUY:	Yes, but why? Why on earth should he do such a thing?
CARTER:	Because someone paid him two hundred quid to do it, that's why. Oh, he's perfectly frank about it, quite brazen in fact.
GUY:	(*Bewildered*) You mean someone actually paid this man two hundred pounds to …
CARTER:	(*Interrupting GUY*) Mr Foster, I'm afraid you've got to prepare yourself for a very unpleasant shock. (*He moves towards GUY*) Your wife was a blackmailer; she worked with a man who called himself Smith. One day they had a quarrel and Smith decided to kill your wife and throw suspicion onto you. He knew that you were tired, overwrought, and that you frequently had rows with Mrs Foster – so it wasn't really very difficult to convey the impression that, apart from being a liar, you were also just a little bit unbalanced. I rather imagine the letter you found, the first letter, must have put even a doubt in your mind about that.
GUY:	My God, how right you are! I'd already told you that I didn't suspect my wife and yet here was a letter from her …
CARTER:	(*Nodding*) Stating that she was having an affair with someone, and that you apparently knew all about it?
GUY:	Exactly! Then when I produced the letter and tried to explain my reasons for going to Elvingdale – the letter was different! You must have thought I was going out of my mind, as well as being a liar.

CARTER: That was certainly what Smith intended us to think.

GUY: You don't think that Smith and Pelham are one and the same person, and he's simply being frank with you at the moment in order to cover up?

CARTER: No, I don't. Pelham's a lone operator, he doesn't get involved in things, not if he can possibly help it. He simply does the job and gets paid for it. I'm pretty sure Miss Stewart operates the same way.

GUY: Carol Stewart?

CARTER: Yes, it's my bet Smith paid her to impersonate your wife and plant that note on the typewriter. You see, the interesting thing is, the first time she telephoned you ...

GUY: The first time?

CARTER: Yes, it wasn't your wife that spoke to you the night she was murdered. It couldn't have been. You received the call at a quarter to eleven, according to the medical report your wife was already dead by then.

GUY: I see. (*Thoughtfully*) Then what exactly happened that night?

CARTER: Mrs Foster came back to get the hatbox; she quietly let herself into the flat while you were working and then ...

The telephone rings. CARTER turns towards the desk. GUY looks at the phone, hesitates, then crosses to the desk and picks up the receiver.

GUY: (*To CARTER*) Excuse me ... (*On the phone*) Guy Foster speaking ...

CUT TO: DOCTOR SWANLEY's Consulting Room, Wimpole Street. Morning.

SWANLEY is sitting at his desk, holding the telephone receiver. He looks tense; drawn.

SWANLEY: Mr Foster, this is Doctor Swanley. I received your letter this morning ...

CUT TO:

GUY: (*Puzzled*) My letter?

GUY looks across at CARTER who is watching him.

CUT TO:

SWANLEY: Yes – don't you think we'd better meet, Mr Foster, and have a talk about this? If you go to the police, well – you know what that means so far as I'm concerned.

CUT TO:

CARTER is now standing next to GUY, listening to the conversation. GUY, still puzzled, looks at the INSPECTOR.

GUY: I'm perfectly prepared to meet you if that's what you want, Doctor Swanley.

CUT TO:

SWANLEY: I think, under the circumstances, it's the best thing to do.

CUT TO:

GUY: All right. What time do you suggest?

The INSPECTOR nods; approving of GUY's decision.

CUT TO:

SWANLEY: I don't think we'd better meet here. I've got an appointment at the Chelsea Hospital this

156

afternoon. Could you possibly meet me on the King's Road somewhere, about four o'clock?

CUT TO:

GUY: Yes, I could do that. There's a café on the corner of Godfrey Street. I'll be there about four. (*A sudden thought*) Oh, and bring my letter, Doctor Swanley. I want it back. (*He replaces the receiver*)

CARTER: (*Looking at GUY*) Why did you ask for the letter?

GUY: Because I didn't send it – and if I'm going to talk about a letter that I didn't send, I'd better find out what's in it.

CARTER: (*Smiling*) I can see you're learning, Mr Foster – learning fast.

CUT TO: The Alcove – a small café in Chelsea. Afternoon.
GUY and DR SWANLEY are sitting in one of the alcoves. GUY is looking at a sheet of notepaper which he holds in his hand. SWANLEY watches him, tense and anxious.
A WAITRESS arrives, puts a pot of tea down on the table and walks away.
GUY looks at SWANLEY, then at the letter again. We see that it is a typewritten letter that bears a quickly scrawled signature – GUY FOSTER – but has no address or date on it. It says:
Dear Doctor Swanley,
I have found a tape recording my wife made – it concerns you and Mary Antrobus. Need I say more? I am taking this to the police unless you tell me the truth. Guy Foster.

SWANLEY: (*Staring at GUY*) What is it you want to know?

157

GUY: (*Tapping the letter*) I've told you what I want to know.

SWANLEY: And if I tell you the truth what happens to the tape?

GUY: If you tell me the truth about the affair, the whole truth, I'll do my best to help you. (*He puts the letter in his pocket*) I can't say more than that, Doctor Swanley.

SWANLEY: Yes, but ... (*Suddenly; tense*) I'll tell you what I'll do! I'll give you three thousand pounds for that tape without even hearing it. Then if you still wish to ...

GUY: (*Stopping SWANLEY*) It's not money I want, Doctor Swanley. (*Shaking his head*) I'm not interested in your money, I just want the facts. Why did you tell the police I consulted you? Why did you deliberately lie about me?

SWANLEY: I – I had to. I was told to do it. Believe me, I had no choice. I was being blackmailed.

GUY: By Miss Dean?

SWANLEY: Yes, and a man I've never met; a man called Smith.

GUY: What happened?

SWANLEY: (*Hesitating, then:*) About a year ago I met Joyce Dean and became infatuated with her. At first, she wouldn't have anything to do with me; then one morning she turned up at my consulting room and asked me to do her a favour. She said a friend of hers, Mary Antrobus, had been taking drugs and she wanted ... (*A shrug*) you can guess what happened. Like a damn fool I supplied her with heroin. A month later I did precisely the same; it was then that Joyce started to

158

	blackmail me. There was just nothing I could do about it. She said that she too was being blackmailed …
GUY:	By whom?
SWANLEY:	By your wife and the man I mentioned – Smith. She said she had to do precisely what they told her. Whether she was telling the truth or not I don't know.
GUY:	Go on …
SWANLEY:	One day she told me that Smith had decided to get rid of your wife and unless I helped him to throw suspicion on to you, he would go to the police about me. You know what happened. They planted a prescription of mine on Mrs Foster and when the police interviewed me …
GUY:	You said I was a patient of yours and that I was mentally ill.
SWANLEY:	(*Nodding*) After the police had interviewed me, I became frightened and refused to supply any more drugs. Mary Antrobus, poor girl, got desperate … In order to stop her from talking, Smith arranged to meet her at your cottage. I don't have to tell you what happened.
GUY:	You say you've never met this man Smith?
SWANLEY:	(*Hesitantly*) No – not to my knowledge. (*Suddenly anxious*) Mr Foster, what are you going to do about that tape? If the police get hold of it then obviously …
GUY:	There isn't a tape.

SWANLEY stares at GUY, astonished.

SWANLEY:	There isn't one?
GUY:	No.

159

SWANLEY: Then what was the point of your letter?

GUY: I didn't write the letter, Doctor.

SWANLEY: (*Agitated; rising*) Then who the hell did?

GUY: (*Quietly*) I don't know. (*He rises*) Doctor Swanley, there's no reason on earth why I should try to help you – but if I were in your shoes, do you know what I'd do?

SWANLEY: No; what would you do?

GUY: I'd go to the nearest phone box, ring up Inspector Carter, and tell him the whole story.

SWANLEY: And what do you think will happen to me, if I do that?

GUY: What's going to happen to you if you don't do it, Doctor Swanley?

SWANLEY looks at GUY for a moment, then with a little nod he turns away from the table and crosses towards the door. GUY stands watching him.

CUT TO: A Quiet Street off the King's Road, Chelsea. Day.
DOCTOR SWANLEY is walking down the street. He is deep in thought, pondering his problem, trying to decide whether to take GUY's advice or not. He reaches the corner of the street and is about to turn into the main road when he notices an empty telephone box on the corner. He looks at the box, hesitates, then suddenly makes a decision and crosses towards it.

CUT TO: Inside the Telephone Box.
SWANLEY is dialling a number. After a little while we hear the number ringing out, then a man's voice comes on the line.

MAN: (*On the other end of the phone*) Whitehall 1212. Scotland Yard ...

SWANLEY: I want to speak to Chief-Inspector Carter, please. My name is Swanley.

MAN: One moment, sir, and I'll put you through.

SWANLEY waits for the extension number and as he does so he becomes aware of the sound of an approaching car. He peers out of the phone box, down the street. The roar of the car grows louder, reaching a crescendo as it races past the box – suddenly there is the noise of revolver shots and the shattering of the phone box window. SWANLEY drops the receiver and clutches his chest. As the noise of the car fades away, he slowly sinks to the floor of the phone box.

CUT TO: The Front Door of GUY FOSTER's Flat. Evening.

DON PAGE is standing at the front door, his finger on the bell button. We can hear the bell ringing inside the flat. DON carries a copy of an evening newspaper and looks slightly on edge. He is glancing at his watch when GUY opens the front door.

GUY: (*Surprised*) Why, hello, Don!

DON: Are you alone, old boy?

GUY: Yes – come in!

DON enters the flat.

CUT TO: The Living Room of GUY's Flat. Evening.

DON enters followed by GUY.

GUY: Would you care for a drink?

DON: No, thanks. (*Hesitantly*) Guy, I don't know whether you've seen the evening paper or not?

GUY: About Swanley? Yes, I've seen it.

DON: What an extraordinary thing! What the devil happened?

GUY: You know what happened, it's in the paper.

DON: Yes, but – (*Indicating the paper*) it says here you were with him just before he was shot.

161

GUY: I was. He asked to see me; I met him in a café on the King's Road.

DON: (*Surprised*) Was Swanley a friend of yours then?

GUY: No, I'd only met him once before. But why are you interested in Dr Swanley? I know you're a patient of his, but he must have a great many patients who …

DON: (*Interrupting GUY*) Look, Guy – I don't want to sound conceited or anything like that, but – well – I'm quite a public figure these days, old boy, and I just can't afford to get mixed up in anything …

GUY: Such as what?

DON: Well – this Swanley business.

GUY: Why should you get mixed up in it? And what exactly is the Swanley business?

DON: (*Irritated*) You know what I mean! You know perfectly well what I mean!

GUY: I'm afraid I don't, Don. Tell me …

DON: If Swanley dies, there'll be an awful lot of questions asked. You'll be interviewed of course and … Well, you're bound to tell them that it was through me that you consulted Swanley in the first place.

GUY: (*Quietly: watching DON*) But I didn't consult him.

DON: You didn't?

GUY: No. (*Smiling*) Don, you can put your mind at rest. If I'm questioned by the press, or anyone else for that matter, I shall tell the truth. And the truth us, I was never a patient of Dr Swanley's. So – (*A shrug*) as far as I'm concerned there's no need for your name to be mentioned.

DON: (*Relieved*) Oh – well, thanks, old boy.

GUY: Is that all you were worried about?

DON: Er – well, frankly, yes …

162

GUY is looking at DON, it is difficult to tell exactly what he is thinking.

GUY: Then don't give it another thought.

DON: (*A shade embarrassed*) Thank you, Guy. (*He looks at his watch again*) I'm afraid I must dash, I promised to be at Paula's by seven o'clock.

DON and GUY move towards the hall.

GUY: Are you having dinner with them?

CUT TO: The Hall of GUY's Flat. Evening.

DON crosses towards the front door, followed by GUY.

DON: No; Felix phoned me this afternoon and asked me to drop round for a drink. Paula's thinking of buying an Aston Martin and she wants to talk to me about it.

GUY: An Aston? That's a pretty fast car.

The door bell rings.

DON: Paula's a pretty fast driver. But she's a jolly good one, I'll say that for her.

GUY opens the front door. CARTER is in the doorway.

CARTER: Good evening, Mr Foster. Could you spare me a moment?

GUY: Yes, of course. Come along in …

GUY moves out into the corridor.

CARTER: (*To Don, as he enters the flat*) Good evening, Mr Page. Is that your Juggernaut outside?

DON: Yes.

CARTER: (*Pleasantly*) Thought so. What'll that do, sir – a hundred miles an hour?

DON: (*To GUY*) He's a little out of date, isn't he, old boy? (*To the INSPECTOR*) She'd do that with a trailer.

CARTER smiles.

163

CUT TO: The Living Room of Guy's Flat. Evening.

GUY enters with the INSPECTOR.

CARTER: What did Mr Page want, sir?

GUY: He'd read about Swanley, and he was frightened his name might be mentioned.

CARTER: (*Puzzled*) Why should he be frightened of that?

GUY: He's a patient of Dr Swanley's and he's very much in the limelight these days.

CARTER: Dr Swanley has a lot of well-known patients. I shouldn't have thought publicity would have worried Mr Page.

GUY: Well, apparently the wrong kind of publicity does.

CARTER: Is there such a thing, sir?

GUY: (*Smiling*) Would you like a drink, Inspector?

CARTER: Thank you. May I have a Scotch and water?

GUY nods and crosses to the drinks table.

GUY: Sit down, Inspector.

The INSPECTOR sits in the armchair: crosses his legs, and eases his shoe. GUY mixes drinks.

GUY: How is Swanley? Is there any news?

CARTER: He's putting up a fight and I've a hunch he's going to make it. I hope so.

GUY: Is he conscious?

CARTER: Yes, he's conscious and he's made a statement. We've already picked up Miss Dean on the strength of it. We're holding her on a blackmail charge. Whether we shall be able to make it stick or not remains to be seen.

GUY crosses to the settee with the drinks.

GUY: Inspector, I've got one or two questions I'd like to ask you.

164

CARTER: I expect you have, sir. (*He takes a glass; smiles*)
            Fire ahead, Mr Foster, I'll tell you anything you
            want to know.

GUY: (*Surprised*) Thank you, Inspector – that's very
            generous of you.

CARTER: Not quite as generous as it sounds, sir. I want
            you to do me a favour ...

GUY: (*Curious*) Oh – what's that?

CARTER: You kick off first, sir.

GUY: Well, I'd like to know about Miss Dean. What
            happened the night she went out to Carlston
            Heath?

CARTER: Smith, the gentleman I've already told you
            about, arranged to meet Miss Dean at The Dial.
            She was getting defiant, a little too sure of
            herself, and he'd decided to get rid of her. Well,
            you know what happened. Miss Dean put up a
            fight and she was lucky. Later, Smith told her
            that if she was prepared to get out of the country,
            he'd leave her alone and do a deal. She agreed.
            Part of the deal was to throw suspicion on to you.

GUY: I see. (*He takes a drink, then:*) Inspector, what
            did you mean the other day when you said – you
            didn't suspect me because I once said ...

CARTER: You said your wife used to buy more hats than
            any other woman you knew, but she never
            seemed to wear one.

GUY: Yes?

CARTER: Mrs Foster deliberately established the fact that
            she was always buying hats. The reason for this
            being that she found it both convenient and safe
            to collect the blackmail money in a hatbox.
            Smith knew this of course.

GUY: (*Puzzled*) Well?

165

CARTER: Well, if you'd been Smith would you have drawn attention to the fact that your wife was frequently seen with a hatbox, although she rarely wore a hat? (*Shaking his head*) I don't think so, Mr Foster. (*He glances at his watch*) But I'll tell you about the hatbox later, sir. Right now, if you don't mind, there's something else I want to talk to you about.

GUY: (*Curious*) Go on, Inspector ...

CARTER: (*He looks at his glass, hesitates, then:*) I want to talk to you about Felix Hepburn, sir.

CARTER looks at GUY.

CUT TO: The Main Room of PAULA HEPBURN's Flat in Eaton Square. Evening.

PAULA, FELIX and DON are having drinks in this consciously elegant drawing room. FELIX is mixing a dry martini whilst DON extols the virtues of his favourite car.

DON: ... Well, all I can say is this, Paula. This friend of mine has done forty-five thousand miles in it and he hasn't even had to decoke ...

PAULA: What's a decoke, darling?

FELIX: Don't be silly, my old dear! (*Turning from the table*) It's no good getting technical, Don – just tell her whether she should buy it or not.

DON: In my opinion, yes. I know it's a fast car, and it's three and a half thousand pounds ...

FELIX: (*Surprised*) Three and a half thousand! (*To PAULA*) I thought you said that jalopy was going to cost about sixteen hundred quid?

PAULA: Don't be absurd, Duckie!

DORA, the maid, appears from the hall.

DORA: (*To PAULA*) Excuse me, madam. Inspector Carter would like to see you.

166

FELIX: Inspector Carter?

DORA: Yes, sir.

PAULA: All right, Dora – show the Inspector in.

DORA goes out.

PAULA: (*To FELIX*) What does he want, I wonder?

FELIX: Haven't a clue, old girl.

DON: I saw him earlier this evening.

PAULA: You did?

DON: Yes, he dropped in on Guy.

CARTER appears in the doorway.

CARTER: I'm sorry to disturb you, Mrs Hepburn, but I'd be most grateful if you could spare me a moment.

The INSPECTOR's manner is faintly apologetic; very friendly.

PAULA: Yes, of course, Inspector.

CARTER: (*To FELIX*) Good evening, sir.

FELIX: Good evening, Inspector.

CARTER: (*Nodding to DON*) Mr Page …

DON: Good evening …

FELIX: (*Indicating the table*) Would you care for a drink?

CARTER: That's very kind of you, but I won't if you don't mind, sir!

FELIX: Please yourself, old man.

PAULA: Did you want to speak to me alone, Inspector?

CARTER: If it's possible, Mrs Hepburn, but I don't wish to inconvenience you in any way.

PAULA: That's quite all right; we'll go into the breakfast room.

PAULA looks at FELIX, then crossing the room opens a door and goes into the adjoining room. With a friendly little nod to both FELIX and DON, the INSPECTOR follows her. As the door closes FELIX turns to DON.

FELIX: (*Faintly annoyed*) Well, that's damn silly, if you like! He must know the old dear will tell me all about it, whatever it is!

DON doesn't say anything; he frowns, and crossing down to the drinks table puts down his glass.

CUT TO: The Breakfast Room of PAULA HEPBURN's Flat in Eaton Square. Evening.

PAULA is sitting on the arm of a chair, CARTER stands facing her.

CARTER: ... Mrs Hepburn, I think perhaps you might be able to help me; and if you can I'd be most grateful if ... Well, if you'd treat the whole matter as confidential – for the time being at any rate.

PAULA: Yes, of course – but how can I help you, Inspector?

CARTER: You and Mrs Foster were very good friends; you saw a great deal of each other ...

PAULA: Why, yes, but you know that ...

CARTER: Did she, at any time, mention a recording she'd made?

PAULA: (*Surprised*) A recording?

CARTER: Yes.

PAULA: (*Shaking her head*) Why, no.

CARTER: Had she a tape recorder?

PAULA: I don't think so. Not to my knowledge.

CARTER: She never spoke to you about one?

PAULA: No.

CARTER: You're sure about that? This is important, Mrs Hepburn.

PAULA: (*Puzzled*) Quite sure.

CARTER: Did you ever see a tape recorder when you visited her flat?

168

PAULA: I don't think so. (*Suddenly*) Wait a minute! I believe Guy had one for a short while, when he was in Fleet Street. He tried it out, but didn't get on with it very well.

CARTER: When was this?

PAULA: Oh – about a year ago.

CARTER: I see. (*Nodding*) Thank you, Mrs Hepburn. (*He holds out his hand*)

PAULA: (*Rising*) Yes, but wait a minute! What's this all about, Inspector?

There is a pause.

CARTER appears to be hesitating, apparently not sure whether to confide in PAULA or not.

CARTER: You've read about Dr Swanley?

PAULA: Yes.

CARTER: We found a letter on him, from Guy Foster. The letter inferred that Mr Foster had a tape recording that had been made by his wife.

PAULA: By Melissa?

CARTER: Yes.

PAULA: Have you spoken to Guy about this?

CARTER: (*Nodding*) I've just left him. He denies having written the letter, he says he knows nothing about the tape.

PAULA: (*Looking at the INSPECTOR*) And you don't believe him?

CARTER: (*After a moment: slowly*) If there's a tape in existence – and personally, I believe there is – then I think Mr Foster's got it. The letter? (*A shrug*) I just wouldn't know. (*Holding out his hand again*) Good night, Mrs Hepburn, I'm sorry to have troubled you.

PAULA slowly shakes hands with the INSPECTOR; she is obviously puzzled.

169

CUT TO: The Kitchen of GUY FOSTER's Flat. Afternoon.
This is a small, well-appointed kitchen with sink unit, table and chairs, Frigidaire, etc. A door leads to the living room and a second door to an outside staircase.

CARTER and DETECTIVE-SERGEANT STAFFORD are sitting at the table drinking tea, there is a tray in front of them complete with a pot of tea and a plate of sweet biscuits. CARTER's pipe and tobacco pouch are on the table.

STAFFORD: (*Sipping tea*) This makes a nice change, sir.

CARTER: I'm glad you think so, Sergeant.

STAFFORD: It isn't that the tea's bad at the Yard, it's just undrinkable.

CARTER: (*Pulling his leg*) Stafford, I shall never understand you. Not in a thousand years. Why should a man of your taste, and undoubted intelligence waste his time in the police force?

STAFFORD: (*Dead pan*) You meet delightful people, sir. Besides, money isn't everything.

CARTER: (*Shocked*) Good God, who told you that?

STAFFORD: The Duke of Portland, sir.

CARTER laughs and at that moment the door bell rings. STAFFORD quickly rises from the table; the blandness has left him. CARTER looks at the SERGEANT, his expression serious. GUY enters from the living room.

GUY: (*A shade tense*) That's the front door …

CARTER: (*Nodding*) You know what to do?

GUY: Yes.

CARTER: Take it easy. Play it nice and cool, sir.

GUY nods and returns to the living room.

CUT TO: The Hall of GUY FOSTER's Flat. Afternoon.
GUY enters the hall and opens the front door. FELIX HEPBURN is standing in the doorway; he wears a camel hair coat and has no hat.

FELIX: Hello, my old dear!

GUY: You're on time, Felix. Come along in!

FELIX: You look tired, Guy. (*He enters the hall*) Have you been working hard?

GUY: Yes, pretty hard.

GUY closes the front door.

CUT TO: The Living Room of GUY's Flat. Afternoon.
FELIX enters, followed by GUY.

GUY: Would you like a drink, or is it too early?

FELIX: I think it's a bit too early for me, old chap.

GUY: How's Paula?

FELIX: Oh, she's fine. Thinking of buying a new car at the moment. Look, Guy, it's no good beating about the bush. I'll tell you why I wanted to see you. That detective chap, Carter, had a word with Paula last night and – well, to cut a long story short, he thinks you're holding out on him.

GUY: Holding out on him?

FELIX: Yes.

GUY: In what way am I holding out on him?

FELIX: Well, he seems to think that Melissa made a tape recording and you've got it nicely tucked away somewhere.

GUY: Why should I have it nicely tucked away somewhere, Felix?

FELIX: Don't ask me, old chap! I don't know. But quite obviously Carter attaches importance to it – great importance.

GUY: (*Quietly; faces him*) And is that what you wanted
             to see me about?
FELIX: Yes. (*He pats Guy's arm*) Guy, my old dear, I
             don't think you understand. You're in a spot. A
             devilishly awkward spot.
GUY: In what way, Felix?
FELIX: The police suspect you! You're the number one
             suspect! If they suddenly find you've got this
             thingymmybob and are holding out of them you've
             had it!
GUY: And what if I haven't got it?
FELIX: Ah, that's a different kettle of fish! That's an
             entirely different story. (*He pats GUY's arm
             again*) Guy, my old dear, Paula and I are worried
             about you – we're only trying to help ...
GUY: Yes, I know, Felix – and I'm very grateful.
The door bell rings.
FELIX: We're meeting Don at five o'clock. We're going
             out to Kingston to take a look at a car.
GUY: Is that the Aston he was telling me about?
FELIX: Yes.
GUY moves towards the hall.
GUY: Excuse me, Felix.
FELIX: You're expecting someone – I'll push off, old
             chap.
GUY and FELIX go out into the hall.

CUT TO: The Hall of GUY FOSTER's Flat. Afternoon.
GUY crosses to the front door followed by FELIX.
FELIX: Now don't forget what I told you! My old man
             always used to say – the gaols are full of people
             who think the police are just a pack of ruddy fools.
*GUY smiles and opens the front door. He is facing DON
PAGE.*

FELIX: (Surprised) Don!

DON stares at FELIX; obviously embarrassed.

DON: (*To FELIX*) I thought we were meeting at the Dorchester?

FELIX: We are at five o'clock. Paula's having her hair done, I'm picking her up in half an hour.

DON: Oh, I see.

GUY: Come along in, Don.

DON: Thanks. (*As he enters the hall:*) See you later, Felix.

FELIX stares at DON, obviously curious about his visit.

FELIX: Yes. (*To GUY*) Bye, old boy.

FELIX walks away as GUY closes the door.

CUT TO: The Kitchen of GUY FOSTER's Flat. Afternoon.

CARTER and the SERGEANT are standing near to the living room. They are listening to GUY and DON; we hear voices from inside the room. The INSPECTOR looks at STAFFORD and gives a little nod. A thick-set man – BOWERS – comes quietly through the other door and, crossing to the INSPECTOR, hands him a note. CARTER glances at it.

CUT TO: The Living Room of GUY's Flat. Afternoon.

GUY is sitting on the arm of the settee staring at DON PAGE who is nervous and ill at ease. He stands near the drinks table.

GUY: ... I'm not sure I understand this, Don. (*He shakes his head*) Are you trying to tell me that ...

DON: I'm trying to tell you that I lied; that I'm very sorry, and I regret it. It's as simple as that.

GUY: You lied about Melissa?

DON: Yes.

GUY: You knew all the time that she was a professional blackmailer and the money she ...

DON: Blackmail? Melissa? Good God, no! Who told you that?

GUY rises and moves towards DON.

GUY: Don, what exactly is it you're trying to tell me?

DON: (*After a moment*) That afternoon – the afternoon you came to see me. You asked me whether Melissa had ever spoken to me about you, about your health. I told you she had. I said she was frightened of you and that I'd advised her to see Doctor Swanley.

GUY: Well?

DON: That wasn't true. Joyce Dean made me say that; she said you'd be getting in touch with me and ...

GUY: She blackmailed you?

DON: Yes. (*A pause, then:*) You remember that accident I had; the taxi driver said I was drunk, but – I got away with it.

GUY: Yes.

DON: (*He nods*) I was tight. I'd had three whiskies on an empty stomach and – well, you know me. When I consulted Swanley, I told him the truth; I told him all about it. I had to. I was in such a hell of a state. Joyce Dean, the little bitch, must have overheard ... (*A shrug*) I'm sorry, Guy, I – I ought to have told you all this before.

GUY: (*Quietly*) Why are you telling me it now?

A pause.

DON doesn't answer.

GUY: You've heard about Joyce Dean, haven't you? You've heard she's been arrested?

DON: Yes.

GUY: So, sooner or later, the chances are, I should have heard about all this anyway?

DON: (*Resenting GUY's tone*) That's one way of looking at it.

174

GUY: What's the other?

DON: (*Facing GUY*) I saw Inspector Carter this morning. I told him my story. I said I'd tell it again if he wanted me to – anytime, anywhere.

GUY looks at DON, then with a friendly little nod, turns away.

GUY: Thank you, Don.

CUT TO: The Kitchen of GUY FOSTER's Flat. Afternoon.

CARTER is alone in the kitchen, leaning against the sink unit, quietly smoking his pipe. GUY enters from the living room closing the kitchen door behind him.

CARTER: Mr Page gone?

GUY: Yes.

GUY takes off his jacket and puts it over the back of the chair.

CARTER: You look worried, sir.

GUY: Well – I am worried. Things aren't working out, are they?

CARTER: They will.

GUY looks at CARTER, then crosses to the fridge and takes out a bottle of milk. He is pouring himself a glass of milk when the phone starts to ring in the living room. He glances across at the INSPECTOR.

CARTER: (*Quietly*) Answer it, sir.

GUY picks up his glass of milk and returns to the living room.

CUT TO: The Living Room of GUY's Flat. Afternoon.

GUY enters from the kitchen. He closes the door behind him, and after putting the glass of milk down on the drinks table, crosses to the desk. He is reaching out for the phone when a voice from the hall says quietly: "Don't answer it"! GUY quickly turns. FELIX is standing in the entrance of the hall; his overcoat over his left arm, an automatic in his right hand. The gun is pointing at GUY.

GUY: (*Quietly*) How did you get in, Felix?

FELIX: I have a key. I've had it for some time, dear boy.

FELIX crosses towards the desk. The phone is still ringing.
GUY looks at it.

FELIX: Let it ring.

There is a pause.

GUY's eyes are on FELIX again. The phone stops ringing.

GUY: What is it you want, Felix?

FELIX: You know what I want. I want that tape – the one
           Melissa made.

GUY: Supposing I told you there wasn't one?

FELIX: (*Quietly*) Guy, I mean business. (*He indicates the
           revolver*) This isn't a toy or a joke …

GUY: I'm sold on that, Felix. But before we discuss the
           tape, there's something I want to know.

FELIX: I didn't come here to discuss …

GUY: I know what you came for, you've already made
           that quite clear!

GUY moves away from the desk and goes towards the table.

GUY: But I don't intend to hand the tape over – I don't
           intend to hand anything over – until you've told
           me exactly what happened.

FELIX: What happened?

GUY: The night you killed Melissa.

FELIX looks at GUY and hesitates.

FELIX: Melissa and I were in business together. I'd
           already made up my mind to get rid of her – she'd
           been spending too much money, drawing attention
           to herself, taking too many risks …

GUY: Go on …

FELIX: (*Suddenly, tensely, revealing an unsuspected
           temper*) What the hell do you mean – go on? I'm
           giving the bloody orders around here!

176

GUY: (*Quietly: ignoring FELIX's outburst*) Tell me
                what happened ...
FELIX: I decided to do it that night! It was a perfect
                opportunity. I told Carol Stewart to get Don
                out of the way, then I made an excuse about
                his phone being out of order and ... I took
                Paula's Volkswagen and met Melissa near
                Holland Park. Almost immediately the stupid,
                silly little bitch started arguing about money,
                and ...

*The phone is ringing again, and FELIX, intensely annoyed at
being interrupted, turns away from GUY and looks towards
the desk. GUY immediately takes advantage of the situation,
swiftly grabbing the glass of milk from the table and tossing
the contents straight into FELIX's face. The gun goes off as
FELIX drops it.*

*CARTER rushes out of the kitchen as GUY searches for the
automatic. FELIX quickly realises what has happened. He
pulls himself together and pushes GUY headlong into the
INSPECTOR. By the time GUY and the cursing CARTER
have sorted themselves out FELIX has vanished into the
bedroom. CARTER rushes to the bedroom door: it is locked
from the inside.*

CARTER: Can he get out that way?
GUY: Only through the window!

*The INSPECTOR nods and races out into the hall. We hear
the front door open and close. GUY hesitates, not quite sure
what to do – then he notices the gun on the floor near the
drinks table. He crosses, picks it up, and quickly returns to the
bedroom door and fires a series of shots into the door lock.
He finally kicks open the door and rushes into the bedroom.*

CUT TO: GUY FOSTER's Bedroom. Afternoon.

GUY bursts into the bedroom, gun in hand – and stops dead. At the far end of the room, FELIX can be seen through the half open window. He is precariously perched on a narrow ledge, desperately attempting to reach the window of an adjoining apartment. He suddenly turns, sees GUY with the gun in his hand, and panics. GUY rushes towards the window as FELIX, with a terrified scream, loses his balance, and falls. GUY stops in his tracks, hesitates, then moves forward and looks out of the window.

CUT TO: The Street outside of GUY FOSTER's Flat. Afternoon.

Looking through the half open window onto the street below, we see the motionless body of FELIX HEPBURN, spreadeagled on the pavement. People are rushing towards the dead man; CARTER, SERGEANT STAFFORD and several uniformed men are already on the scene. Two police cars arrive, braking to a standstill near where the INSPECTOR is standing. CARTER looks across at one of the new arrivals and shakes his head.

CUT TO: The Living Room of GUY FOSTER's Flat. Evening.

A suitcase containing clothes and one or two books is on the settee. GUY comes out of the kitchen with the INSPECTOR. He crosses to the drinks table and picks up the INSPECTOR's tobacco pouch and pipe.

GUY: Here we are – I found them in the kitchen.

CARTER: Thank you, sir.

The INSPECTOR puts the pipe and pouch into his pocket.

CARTER: You'll be interested to know we've been through Mr Hepburn's flat. He had thirty thousand pounds – in cash.

178

GUY:	But Felix always made out he was broke. I thought it was Paula that had the money.
CARTER:	That's what most people thought, sir – and he encouraged the idea by telling everyone he was hard up. (*Shaking his head*) It's funny, you know, but – people are always prepared to accept the stupid man with the wealthy wife.
GUY:	But hadn't Paula any money of her own?
CARTER:	No, sir, not a bob – she simply worked for her husband and did as she was told. (*Significantly*) Precisely as she was told. (*He crosses towards the hall*) Swanley's getting better. I was on to the hospital this afternoon. He's off the danger list. He's a damn good doctor that man, it's a terrible pity he ran into this kind of trouble.
GUY:	Yes, I agree. (*Puzzled*) Inspector, who sent him that letter, the one with my name on it, the one about the tape recorder?
CARTER:	(*Vaguely; curiously disinterested*) I don't know, sir.
GUY:	It was nonsense, you know. Melissa never even had a tape recorder.
CARTER:	I'm sure you're right, sir.
GUY:	(*Looking at CARTER*) Of course, if Swanley hadn't received that letter, he would never have made a statement; and Felix Hepburn, I imagine would still be in business.
CARTER:	Right again, sir. (*He deliberately changes the subject by indicating the suitcase*) Going far, Mr Foster?

GUY: I'm going down to Cornwall. A friend of mine has got a house near St Ives and he's invited me to stay with him.

CARTER: A very good idea. You'll probably work much better down there. (*He holds out his hand*) Goodbye, and good luck.

GUY: Thank you.

GUY and CARTER shake hands, and CARTER crosses towards the hall.

GUY: Oh, Inspector ...

CARTER: (*Turning*) Yes, sir?

GUY: I suppose – you didn't send that letter, by any chance?

CARTER: (*Horrified*) Me, sir?

GUY: (*Smiling*) Yes, you, Inspector.

CARTER: Good Lord, whatever gave you that idea? The police can't use those sort of tactics, sir. The criminal classes just wouldn't stand for it. (*He shakes his head*) You can put that idea right out of your head, Mr Foster!

With a friendly wave CARTER goes out into the hall. GUY smiles and crossing to the desk, collects a manilla folder, several pens, and the manuscript of his novel. He takes these across to the suitcase, then returns to the desk. He is putting the cover on his typewriter when his eye catches the photograph of MELISSA. The smile slowly fades as he stares at the photograph; after a momentary hesitation he picks it up.

The camera tracks into a close-up of the photograph in GUY's hand. We see the word MELISSA scrawled across the photograph.

THE END

Press Pack

... press cuttings about Melissa

Thriller

Tony Britton will be one of the first stars to be seen regularly on BBC2, the new television service which opens in April.

He has the main part in the latest Francis Durbridge serial, *Melissa* – one of the top Sunday-evening attractions.

The opportunity is particularly attractive because he is such a fan of the Durbridge serials. Says Mr Britton: "This is one for adult audiences. Durbridge constructs his stories like a solidly-built house, architecturally interesting on different levels, with twisting passages, leading to strange old rooms."

Tony Britton, 39, began his acting career in amateur drama in Weston-super-Mare. He made his tv debut in 1952 and in the course of 30 plays has built himself into one of tv's favourite leading men.

Evening News

Francis Durbridge serial – but millions won't see it
by **Roy Wilson**

Is it simply a case of sour grapes? I am not at all sure, but I couldn't help feeling a twinge of annoyance ...? resentment ...? disappointment ...? childishly, perhaps – when I was reading about BBC2 this week.

Michael Peacock, BBC2 Chief of Programmes, was saying that he had just watched the recording of the first drama programme for the new channel, opening on 625 lines in the London area in April.

Why should I feel any annoyance ...? resentment ...? disappointment ...? about what?

Because Mr Peacock went on to say that the first BBC2 production to go into the can was a new Francis Durbridge serial.

Now, Francis Durbridge may not be everybody's favourite, but he's one of mine, and his serials are the most fascinating and craftsmanlike in their own particular field.

Mr Durbridge's name is synonymous with absorbing, exciting television thriller entertainment, and his serials are invariably talking-points among viewers from the first instalment.

Mr Peacock says that this new Durbridge serial lined up for BBC2, *Melissa*, is one of the finest he has ever written.

Nobody can blame Mr Peacock for shopping in the best market, for his job is to make BBC2 a success from the word go. No serial could have a stronger pull during the first vital weeks of the new service's existence.

But what about the millions of viewers who will be unable to see BBC2 for years to come? They will probably have to wait a long time for the next Durbridge serial on BBC1. There must be a limit to even that prolific writer's output.

This question of supply and demand in the provision of material for BBC1 and BBC2 revives one of my earliest fears. Is there going to be enough to keep both services going?

And isn't the standard of some of it now proof that there's a real shortage of quality output?

Divide the good stuff by two, and BBC1 which is what most of us will be seeing for two or three years more, will be only half as good.

Somebody suggested to me the other day that the writers will emerge to meet the need. But will they?

So far, neither BBC nor ITV has managed to find enough. The serials, the plays, the comedy shows turn up, but comparatively few turn up trumps.

182

How much is going to be absorbed by BBC2 that should have come our way on BBC1? For a start it looks as if we shall be at least a Francis Durbridge serial short. Who can tell what else we shall miss is the many months ahead?

Eastern Evening News

First of a Series

Melissa will be the first of a new series of 'adult' crime and adventure serials on BBC2. Written by ace thriller writer Francis Durbridge, it stars Tony Britton as a journalist who only wants to settle down quietly and write books, but who finds himself tragically and personally involved in a web of intrigue and crime.

Taking time off from rehearsals recently, Tony said: "I find it very difficult to put into words my admiration for Francis Durbridge – he is the master of the thriller serials. He constructs them like a solidly-built house, architecturally interesting on different levels, with twisting passages leading to odd and strange rooms.

"He never telegrams where the plot may lead to next and, just when the story seems to be taking a straightforward course, he will slap you in the face with a fabulous cliff-hanger situation that just forces you to switch on for the next episode."

Co-starring with Tony is Helen Christie, who is playing in her first thriller serial. "It certainly adds to the interest and excitement when even the cast doesn't know what the outcome of the story will be," she says. "The tension in the studio builds up as we see the scripts week to week and try to guess who the criminal might be. It might be me! It's just like being one piece of a jigsaw puzzle, each piece gradually falling into place."

My View Last Night by **Bob Miller** (contains spoilers)

The Francis Durbridge serial *Melissa* is designed to shock and quicken the pulse, but nothing in last night's episode achieved that effect quite so well as the announcement that preceded it. Just as millions were settling down in anticipation a correct BBC voice said – "There now follows a repeat of *Meeting Point.*"

For an awful moment I thought the programme schedule had been rearranged, but it was the announcer's mistake, not mine. Melissa followed, as expected, and if it sagged a bit in the middle it was no wonder after the hectic goings on of the past three weeks. Towards the end, however, it came away strongly and ended with another of Durbridge's dumbfounding cliff-hangers – If this is George Antrobus, who was the man who came running into Guy Foster's flat with a gun?

Glasgow Evening Times

Sunday night audience stealer by **John Corbyn**

Everyone's talking about the BBC new Sunday night serial *Melissa*.

Not because it is a programme that is different – and 'different' programmes are few and far between – but it is because it is in the familiar Francis Durbridge pattern.

Whodunnit addicts go a real bundle on Francis Durbridge serials, which are one of the BBC's biggest attractions, so much so that one wonders why we don't have more of them.

For Francis Durbridge has become to BBC television what Alfred Hitchcock is to the cinema: a master of suspense and an adroit manipulator of situations and characters.

After making his name on steam radio, he came to the fore with a number of BBC weekly serials, including *The*

184

Scarf and three separate versions of *The World of Tim Frazer*, which established him as a master of detective serials.

Durbridge's talent lies in several directions. He makes the most outlandish situations sound plausible and everyday; his characters are finely drawn and easily recognisable as the man in the train, the girl in the shop, or the boss in the office; his policemen are faithful to life, never caricatures or overdrawn; his red herrings are never so fantastic so as to annoy when we realise we swallowed the bait; the solution is invariably logical and sensible and never involves out-of-the-fringe characters, the episodes are often authentically filmed on easily-recognisable locations; and each episode ends on such a high pitch of excitement and tension that it becomes an absolute "must" for us not to miss the next instalment. In short, he mesmerises.

This being so, it is difficult to understand why the BBC are so niggardly in handling out such excellent and popular fare.

The current series, *Melissa*, was made for BBC2 and comes to BBC1 as an afterthought and a useful filler for summer nights, not the best of viewing periods.

Yet it is a more compulsive viewing attraction than almost any other BBC programme. I know viewers who refuse to leave home on Sunday nights in case they should miss an episode (this despite the fact that it is being screened as late as 10.25) and another who insists on being in front of the telly when the next instalment is due, no matter where she may be.

For a long time now, ITV have monopolised Sunday nights one way and another and the BBC never seem to have taken the fact seriously.

The Francis Durbridge serials could be one answer to this popularity, and the BBC must have some inkling of this for they have timed the new serial to draw viewers away from the long-running *Armchair Mystery Theatre*.

But it's a pity they don't take the challenge a little more seriously. Then the Durbridge-starved viewers could have more of their favourite fare without having to wait months on end for BBC "seconds" and ITV might find their Sunday night audience dwindling.

Brighton Evening Argus

When Your Friends Come Between You and Melissa
by **Jim Webber**

Francis Durbridge is a master of the cliff-hanger suspense serial and *Melissa* now being screened on BBC1 is right up to the maestro's form.

This was made for BBC2 and is now being repeated on the first channel, for which many thanks, but as with all such serials it poses a pretty problem for the viewer.

There is absolutely nothing worse than missing one episode for reasons beyond one's control. Friends may decide unexpectedly to drop in and politeness necessitates a turning off of the television set.

And the social niceties have to be observed despite the growing frustration of knowing that while this is going on one complete episode of the serial which has compelled one's viewing for weeks is now slipping into limbo.

It is not so bad with the long runners, for the story line progresses so slowly that one can, if one wishes, easily catch up.

But in the *Melissa* type, the six-part serials, it can be fatal. Especially if it is a mystery by Mr Durbridge who dispenses his clues and red herrings with unerring skill, carefully sparing them.

Admittedly it would run some two and a half hours, but I guarantee this would be absorbing viewing on, say, a Sunday afternoon. And of a quality to completely put in the shade

186

many of the dusty old films that are resurrected and slotted in to ninety minutes or more of repeat time.

It could be argued that two and a half hours is too long for one show. But not, I feel with Mr Durbridge having written it. The surprises, the twists, are so adroitly manoeuvred that the author maintains an air of tension as taut as a bowstring.

Careful editing could piece the episodes together so neatly that one could settle back to the promise of the complete show, free from the anxiety of missing part of it, a danger always present if the run is extended to a period of weeks.

There are many other serials that have been screened in the past that could well be repeated in a telescoped form and I guarantee that their standard would be miles above many of those old movies that were tenth rate when they were made, let alone museum pieces nowadays.

Yet both channels still scrabble around unloading them on to us when television itself is now of an age when programmes of quality, made by tv for tv, could surely be resurrected?

Bristol Evening Post

My View Last Night by **Bob Addison** (contains spoilers)

What a relief! At last I managed to get a good Sunday night's sleep – something that's evaded me these past six Sundays. Today I woke up refreshed. The reason: Felix Hepburn, before committing suicide, confessed to murdering Melissa, his former partner in a lucrative blackmail business.

And so ended *Melissa* – another Francis Durbridge serial so packed with intrigue, excitement, and drama that its ending left one gasping. Well, did you guess who the murderer was?

There was just one mystery left, however. Who was telephoning Guy Foster when Felix stopped him answering it …? Incidentally did you notice Guy had a glass of milk last night instead of countless glasses of whisky? The past six worrying weeks must have started an ulcer!

Those sleepless nights apart, I shall miss *Melissa*!

Glasgow Evening Times

Tony Keeps a Secret that Intrigues Millions
by **Gordon Hislop**

Life is hazardous these days for Tony Britton. Outside the theatre, in the street, in the shops, he is stopped and asked: "Tell us, Mr Britton, who did it? Was it you?"

It started when *Melissa*, Tony's thriller series, was screened, giving some urgency to Sunday night viewing. "The reaction," he tells me, "has been terrific.

"When they ask who the murderer is I get away by pleading the Official Secrets Act.

"Amazing. Especially as it's the third time round for the series. It's already been twice on BBC2. It shows what a market there is for a well-written cliff-hanger.

"I was one of the few to know early on who the killer was to be. But only because I insisted. I thought I could smell a bit of character development when I read the first script. Knowing the ending would help me.

"But I was the only one to know. The rest of the cast were kept in the dark. That's the way the author, Francis Durbridge works. We used to get the next week's script when we had recorded the previous instalment. All frightfully hush hush."

Scottish Sunday Express

Rolls in view

Francis Durbridge's thriller Melissa now being shot for West German television set German director Paul May a poser.

The script called for a Rolls-Royce and, since the action was set in England, it has to be a Rolls with right-hand drive.

May, who is shooting the three-part series in the Cologne area, combed the Federal Republic before he ran one to earth in Southern Germany.

Its rich owner agreed to loan his limousine, but on one condition – that his chauffeur should have a role in the play.

May accepted and an anticipated 20 million viewers will see both Rolls and driver when the series is screened next January.

Evening News

What Melissa Did by Pendennis

Francis Durbridge's televised thriller serial Melissa has even made its mark on German politics.

In Kulmbach, a small Bavarian town famous for its beer, the Christian Socialist Party has made a pact with the neo-Nazis for today's local elections, and it was all Melissa's fault. The local party met in a pub to discuss tactics the night Durbridge's thriller was being shown on television, and nobody wanted to miss a minute of it. When the question of the alliance was put they all voted "Yes" and hurried into the bar to watch the programme.

Francis Durbridge commented: "I only set out to entertain. I find that difficult enough without getting involved in politics."

The Observer

189